The howl of cheated warriors breaking over them, Eli and the Oglala girl thundered out of camp. Before they hit the creek, White Doe swung close and handed an astonished Eli his Remington.

Once Eli was sure they were out of sight he reined in and changed directions. Walking, the horses could not be heard for any distance and the new moon was not due to rise until well into morning, besides he had no desire to injure either of the horses and he was getting lightheaded. The fugitives rode in silence for several miles before White Doe noticed Eli begin to slump in his saddle. She gigged her horse and took Sonny's reins, pulling in both animals, then dismounted and clambered up behind Eli, whose protests she ignored.

"Tall Bear is wounded," she stated. "We go to a place to treat him."

"I have to get back to the fort." He had to warn the general, the settlers had to be brought in. Everyone must be told that Wild Dog's war path would soon lead him against whites.

"You know," White Doe began, interrupting the scout's train of thought. "There are many ways a woman can heal a man . . . ."

#13
THE SCOUT
OGLALA OUTBREAK

BY
BUCK
GENTRY

ZEBRA BOOKS
KENSINGTON PUBLISHING CORP.

ZEBRA BOOKS

are published by

KENSINGTON PUBLISHING CORP.
475 Park Avenue South
New York, N.Y. 10016

First printing: November, 1983

Printed in the United States of America

This book is dedicated to *David Taylor*, author and scholar, with sincere thanks for his invaluable help.

BG

We took away their country, broke up their mode of living, their habits of life, introduced disease and decay among them, and it was for this and against this that they made war. Could anyone expect less?
—Gen. Phillip Sheridan

Scouting is a congenial profession leading to a terrible death.
—George Armstrong Custer

Chapter One

Blazing summer sun had warmed the air along the creek bank where the concentric rings of tipis had been raised. Some of the Oglala women worked diligently on the evening meal, while others washed clothing in the creek, pounding the garments on rocks. Naked children ran laughing through the camp squealing the joys of innocence.

The *eyanpaha;* the village crier, ran past the three concentric circles of the village hoop, bellowing in a voice loud enough to shake the buffalo hide on the tipis, relishing his all important purpose.

"Riders, brothers of the Oglala, come to our camp! Painted for war!"

Every horse, dog and Indian heard the *eyanpaha* as he ran through the lodges to the sparse tree line that shaded the pony herd. He then returned to a large lodge at the center. Painted with fierce reds and yellows, enhanced by strong shades of blue, it was obviously the dwelling of a man of great importance. He scratched at the entrance, and when bid to do so, slid into the dark interior.

Riders burst from cover on a rise the other side of the creek, their horses foam-flecked. They charged across the shallow creek, throwing sheets of water up from the rocky bed.

"Make way!" shouted a warrior from his wild-eyed pony. "Wild Dog comes with his death song!"

"Ayeeah!" The one known as Wild Dog screeched, shaking his Winchester over his head as he slid to a halt near the center of camp. His face was lean and drawn like a sick man, eyes sunk far back in his head and his hawk nose pointed toward the gathering throng. "Hear me, people of Oglala. I have had a vision. I have dreamt of the earth scourged of all white men!"

Wild Dog's eyes glowed like the embers of a wind-whipped fire, his face twisted into a spirit mask that sent chills through the young warriors. A young eagle shrilled in the sky above, and Wild Dog jerked his head to look heavenward.

"Wambli gleska!" The young war chief started singing, calling to the spirit of the bird. *"Oyate nimkte wacin yelo*—the people shall live."

Wild Dog's voice sounded like water laughing as it slid along the creek, playing with the smooth rocks it fell over. A beautiful, soothing voice saying comforting things, and many were impressed. Then he continued with another song, and it spoke of many things, a list of towns where white men dwelt on the plains. He abruptly stopped his song.

"I have had a vision," he explained. "In it I heard this song, a death song that went on for many moons, but that ended. The death song was many verses, a death poem for every white man on the land!"

Black Spotted Horse strode majestically from his lodge, carrying his Winchester rifle in one hand, a medicine bundle in the other. The leader of this band of Oglala counted many winters on himself, yet his bronzed flesh rippled with tough muscle and he sported scars from many battles. His wide face and curved nose had few wrinkles to herald his advanced

8

age. He sighed softly while screwing his face into a scowl to hide his thoughts.

Another great warrior chief out to conquer the land, he thought sourly. Wild Dog could not claim to be the first to have visions of himself as a mighty war leader who was destined to rid the earth of the round-eyes. Sadly he would not be the last.

"Ho, Wild Dog!" Black Spotted Horse shouted abrasively. "Are you so arrogant that you enter a camp without calling upon its leader? Have you no time for courtesy?"

"I have no time for resistance to my vision," Wild Dog shouted back. "I want you to join me in my destiny."

Now the older warrior smiled. Where else to denounce this deluded one, re-named after the dog with foam in its mouth, but in the meeting place. His own eloquence there would keep his young braves away from Wild Dog. In the sacred ritual of council where one must listen, if one wished to be heard, his words would weigh heavily, while those of the young upstart would sound hollow. He turned to the gathered band and threw his hands over his head.

"Prepare meat for a visitor feast. Erect the great lodge."

An hour later, Wild Dog stood first before the council fire. His turbulent eyes and face, with war paint smeared on his rippling chest made him look all the more demonic. He did not speak to an audience receptive to his message. The young bucks grunted in encouragement, but few present believed the elimination of the white man was possible, or even desirable.

"The white-eye is a spoiler of the land, perverter of the people. He kills without thought, and herds us like his cattle. His given word melts as snow. Many

9

summers ago I had a vision, the vision I told you. I went back to that dream many times, each time learning more of my song, until I know it all. A kill song for every white man on the land, for a six days ride in any direction from our land."

Wild Dog began to sing. He sang of infinite power, a medicine song calling upon the spirits of the four directions and the heavens, even the Earth Mother to bear witness. The spellbinder demanded aid from the spirits of wind, rain and thunder. He prevailed upon the ruling specters of bear, coyote and *pte;* the buffalo. Ending his song, Wild Dog made a speech laced with a mystic hatred, addressing the feral natures of his audience. Crying to the love of the land in their hearts, he launched a tirade upon the destructive and deceitful nature of the enemy; the hated but feared *wasicun.* Wild Dog's eyes gleamed with the power of his words, hysterical joy trilled behind his beautiful voice, while his mesmerizing, irresistible presence swelled over the people.

By contrast, Black Spotted Horse remained calm, his self possession rocklike and enduring. When his time came to speak, his words were sane and calming, he marshaled facts and built with them, as a master mason would use bricks to fashion a structure strong and lasting, that those who look upon it may witness truth.

"Wild Dog says he knows the death song for every white on the land. If a real thing, it is powerful medicine. Yet, all die, even whites die. Does this 'great warrior' plan to go where the whites build great lodges, one upon another and are more numerous than the blades of grass upon the prairie? Will our medicine singer strike them all down in their vast numbers? *No!* I say that many shall die, here on our lands they shall die and many will be white. But many

10

more shall be red. If this man has powerful medicine he may stir the Great White Father in Washington to send all his soldiers against the Oglala. Can the mightiest warrior destroy an anthill by stamping upon it? Our braves may destroy many times many, yet the Oglala will no longer ride the plains. There will be no Oglala!"

He leaned to the light of the worlds. He called upon no spirit, sang no song, but communicated with his people as only a true, caring leader can. In the end it was he who had won.

Wild Dog had traveled to many bands, many peoples had listened to his song and taken it to burn in their own hearts with dark malevolence. Nowhere had he encountered such a presence as Black Spotted Horse who called his people from the brink of the abyss that Wild Dog prepared for them.

Suddenly the potent medicine that ran so constantly in his head, and made him rock to its rhythm even as he sat, revealed to him a new song, an urgent song to be fulfilled now!

Wild Dog responded instantly to the new direction, as he had promised he would. He leaped to his feet, the mystic song bursting in his throat. In his hand a razor-edged tomahawk.

It was an unpolished assault, totally devoid of the style and grace of the truly great warrior. The mighty Black Spotted Horse calmly reacted to the attack with a sweeping arc of his hand to lead his antagonist away and into the dirt, to where he can never regain honor for this low and despicable act.

Whether by madness, blind luck or the capricious intervention of a spirit from Wild Dog's song, he did not go where he had been directed. By some legerdemain that no eye could follow, the war hatchet quivered in the breast of Spotted Horse. The very violence and the horror of sacrilege froze the witnesses of the murder until the mad chief folded his arms upon his chest and resumed his song.

When Spotted Horse fell dying to the floor of the council lodge, indignation pulled the shocked men to their feet. Even then, the song held them rooted. Stalking through the frozen ranks, the murderer remained as untouchable as a mere apparition, his face a mask of demonic arrogance as he raised his voice in communion with the dark powers he served.

The followers of Wild Dog turned at once and followed in lockstep with their master to the waiting ponies. They mounted in silence. Nearly half a dozen of the village's younger warriors ran to gather up their favorite ponies and weapons while their families looked on in stony faced disapproval. The wives of the fallen chief set up a shrill keening while they ran to his side, one already hacking at her braids. The outlaws, both old and new recruits turned to the East and left the shocked, leaderless camp. Only then did Wild Dog stop the deadly song to shout a warning. "All who oppose me shall share the fate of Black Spotted Horse."

Usually the air hung like a wet, hot blanket along the banks of Loadstone Creek two miles from Fort Rawlins. In the still of early morning though, and in the shade of a lone pine that somehow found its way to the edge of the slow moving stream, some comfort could be found. Eli Holten, chief scout for the 12th U.S. Cavalry watched his line anxiously while his belly growled. He'd been there since first light and couldn't boast a nibble.

He looked from under the brim of his floppy hat, heels dug into the clay bank, and studied the other

12

side. He gazed out across the rolling, grassy prairie and sparse trees. His many years of living with the Sioux had trained his eyes to look and see, instead of assume what was there.

A twig snapped above and behind him. Eli rolled like a cat, his big Remington slid from leather to hand without conscious volition. The scout went up the bank like a snake, shedding his hat in the process and froze motionless, no more than his eyes over the crest.

A bright smiling face with pink cheeks and white teeth looked down at him.

"Boo!" the young blonde exclaimed, her full red lips lingering in the heart shape needed for the word.

Eli rose from the bank and cautiously stood, looking for anyone else who might be around.

"Don'cha remember me Mr. Holten?" the girl asked as she began struggling down the bank. "We met last night at the dance."

The scout recalled her all right. The delectable but gushy little doll who caused the row with his current amore, which led to a retreat from the dance and the subsequent all night poker session in General Corrington's office. She was also the reason, due to the chain of events, that he was broke and fishing for his breakfast.

"Sure I know you, you're Sally Sue," Eli responded, studying the tired looking bay gelding she had tied to a piece of scrub in a swale where his own Morgan, Sonny could not see him. According to the sweat marks the bay had not carried double.

"Sally Sue Hearst." The girl qualified with a curtsey.

"A little way from the wagon train aren't ya?" the scout inquired.

"Oh yes," the girl bubbled, her big blue eyes laughing as she drew closer. "I rode out here all by myself. I . . . Ah I asked about you at the Fort. That nice sergeant, ya know, the one with the big belly, said you'd probably be fishing out here this morning. I just decided to ride out and visit."

Shit, thought Holten, this will be all over the post by now. Ah well, probably wouldn't be any chance of patch . . .

A sudden violent swirl in the creek distracted him. Breakfast!

Eli fell on the willow pole, already tasting broiled catfish.

"I guess it was jest plain foolish ta' take off like that," Sally Sue continued, oblivious of the confrontation occurring. "But I'm eighteen years old 'n I c'n take care of myself, 'n besides I knew you'd be out here, Mr. Holten." This Gatling gun burst came as she leaned toward Holten from her position above and a little behind him.

Eli Holten was an Army scout, not a sport fisherman. His pole had been cut on the spot and equipped with a short stout line and an improvised hook. When Eli grabbed the pole, he knew that if he was to land breakfast it'd have to be before the fish could spit his hook out. So, as soon as he decided the creature had swallowed the hook, Eli heaved it ashore.

Sally Sue had caught her breath and launched into . . . "Ya know, I been admirin' ya Eli, since we—"*WHAP!*

The slimy bullhead sailed past Eli's shoulder even as he reacted. His counter-effort reversed the fish's course but not before the tail slapped Sally Sue full in the face.

Things happened kind of fast then. Eli continued to swing the fish all the way around until he could fling pole and all over the bank while Sally Sue lost her balance and fell butt-first in the mud.

"Aargh! Yick!" Sally exclaimed. "Yuck, I've been kissed by a fish."

Eli dropped to his knees and examined Sally Sue's face for barbel punctures. Seeing none, he climbed the bank and retrieved breakfast, which he placed on a stringer and carefully anchored it to a protruding pine root. By this time the girl had begun to blubber so the scout returned to her and proceeded to mop some of the fish slime from her lips.

"Humph," he grunted. "Looks to me more like you done the kissin', the fish was wrong end to."

"Get my cheeks," she begged. "Sheesh! I can clean 'em, I can cook 'em and I can eat 'em, but I sure draw the line at kissin' 'em . . . either end!"

"Now I sure am sorry." Eli laughed, the humor of the moment getting the best of him.

"Behind my ears," she whimpered, drawing her face up closer to his.

"How'd it get behind your ears?" Holten asked.

The girl wrapped her arms around the scout's back. "It didn't," she chortled. "I jest wanted you to play with my ears."

Eli stopped wiping. Sally Sue smiled impishly up at him. Holten felt a familiar urge in his groin and slowly smiled back.

"That why you're here?" he queried.

"I got a powerful urge for you Eli," the girl answered, her blue eyes smoky. She pulled up closer to Eli's face and her tongue flicked out to his lips before he could open his mouth to exchange the sensual act. He slipped his arms behind her back and under her legs, then lifted her in his arms.

"Let's go over here, up the bank," he told her. "There's a nice grassy spot where I can have breakfast—later."

"Hurry Eli," Sally Sue begged, her lush breasts

15

stretching at the material restricting them.

Holten walked along the bank, his pants tightening with anticipation.

Sally Sue cuddled into the crook of his arm like a puppy as he laid her on the grass. She obligingly rolled a bit to one side so the scout could unbutton her dress, then slid the garment off her shoulders, her back to Eli as she pushed it down past her hips. When Sally Sue kicked free of her dress, Holten could see she wore no undergarments.

Smilingly she spread her beautiful thighs, then dropped a hand to massage the furry mound of flesh between them. Eli found trouble breathing as he watched the moist pink petals of her passion flower blossom wide.

Eli scrambled to his feet, stripping his moccasins as he rose and began fumbling at his belt.

"I'll get the pants," Sally Sue cooed as she came to her knees before Holten. "You take care of the shirt."

She got the trousers open with practiced ease but fell back when his long, thick manhood sprang free.

"Lordy Eli!" she cried, then leaned hesitantly forward, the magnificent erection thrusting into the bright yellow hair on her shoulder as she slid his cords the rest of the way down. Eli stepped out of his breeches and threw his flannel shirt to one side.

Sally Sue paused only long enough to smile up at the scout, then she leaned back across the shaded grass and spread her legs, wide. Her firm large breasts flattened slightly as she lay prone, but the pink, swollen nipples pointed at Eli like bullets and he could feel them against his hairy chest as he covered the satin skinned body with his own.

With both hands Sally Sue reached down and directed Eli's huge phallus into the small portal between her legs, scantily covered by silky blonde

16

pubic hair. Inch by careful inch Holten advanced the iron hard spear into her body.

"Uhh! . . . Ohh!! Eli!" Sally Sue's loving protest heightened his pleasure as he worked steadily into the mercilessly tight tunnel, the struggle bringing his pleasure to a painful intensity.

By the third stroke of his massive organ, Sally Sue was gushingly wet and relaxed enough to take the whole thing.

"Oh God, how good it is!" By the fifth thrust Sally Sue's hips developed a motion of their own, throwing her dripping sex at the plunging rod.

Squealing her joy, Sally's gyrations became wilder as her skillful muscles quivered and clasped at the huge device that plunged far, far into her. She grunted deep appreciation, like a foraging pig with each inward thrust and moaned painful loss to the out-stroke.

Eli began to pick up the rythmn, the synchroniza-tion sending a mutual, spine-tingling shock of pleasure coursing just beneath their skins.

"Oh! . . . Oh! . . . Oh! OH!" Sally redoubled her efforts until the familiar pretty lights began to burst in her head. Her spirit fled her body and she contracted mightily, while her sanity escaped in a wild howl of pure animal pleasure.

Eli felt the floodgates strain under the pressure of his passion as the slippery little tunnel squeezed impos-sibly tight. Sensation hovered on the brink of pain as he spurted out his life-force, then scaled down slowly at each release. By this time Sally was well over the brink and the huge phallus was drawing a strained . . . "Aaagh . . . Aagh, Agh," that kept her lover pumping an extra stroke or so.

They lay panting and entwined for some time before Eli's hunger sent him after his catfish breakfast.

The scout broiled the single fish to a golden color. Both he and Sally Sue moved about the fire in the raw, though she did throw her dress across her shoulders as a precaution against sunburn.

"There's not much to eat," Eli apologized as he prepared to cut the fish in half on his tin plate and divide it up.

"Oh don't worry about me." Sally giggled. "I already had breakfast. You just sit down next to this tree here." She directed him to lean against the cottonwood under which they had made love. "I'll just amuse myself like this."

She dropped to her knees and swallowed the scout's flaccid manhood in a single gulp. When the rapidly hardening shaft began to push her head back, she extracted it long enough to smile impishly up at Holten.

"Eat your breakfast sweetheart, don't mind me."

It made quite a distraction, but somehow Eli managed to finish the catfish with doubled appreciation.

The ride back to the Fort proved a pleasant enough trip. The girl asked about life on a military post, what the men did to amuse themselves. She seemed particularly interested in pay rates and job security.

"Sounds like you are looking for a husband," Eli teased.

Sally Sue smiled, though her eyes remained inscrutable. From a distance the high, palisaded walls of Fort Rawlins blended with the plains. Thin tendrils of white smoke rose from morning fires and when the two riders drew closer, Holten could see a solitary figure pacing back and forth above the main gate. Off to the left, a circle of wagons were encamped, recuperating from their long journey and preparing to move on.

"I better be getting back to my folks," Sally sighed.

"I'll have lots of chores to do." She smiled possessively at the scout, studying his face. "Sometime real soon I'd like ya' ta meet my family."

"Oh . . . I, ah, I reckon you'll be gone before I get a chance for that." Holten replied, in hopes of setting the record straight. He was definitely not available.

"I imagine so," Sally returned, her voice going kind of flat. She suddenly stabbed her bay with slippered heels and headed for the wagons at a gallop. Eli sighed relief and rode on to the Fort, still hungry.

Sally Sue dropped her nag to a trot a little shy of the train. Not a bad catch she thought, recalling the scout's powerful body, rugged features and wonderfully huge endowment. Not bad at all for a sixteen-year-old who had missed two periods.

Reining her horse to a walk, she guided it to where her father and four husky brothers greased the wheels of one of the Conestogas that carried commercial goods with the train.

"Daddy," the lovely young blonde cried as she slid from the saddle to throw herself into his arms. She hugged his barrel chest and repeated, "Oh Daddy."

"What is it Sally Sue?" asked her oldest brother, Matthew, deep concern wrinkling his simple forehead.

"Oh Daddy," wailed Sally Sue to her doting father. "Have I got something to tell you . . ."

Chapter Two

Eli Holten carefully studied the hostile ground he had to cover to reach safety. A hunted man could take no chances. The parade ground in the midday sun of summer had only swirls of dust to challenge him. Still the scout used all of his many years of experience to make sure his path was clear. A knot formed in his stomach as he dared step out into the light from the stable's cover. His goal was General Corrington's office. He'd been ordered to report.

Nervously, glancing both ways, the scout broke into bright sunlight at a dead run in a single stride. Leaping a water trough, he dodged the well structure and lined out for the flag pole. As it flashed past he felt a surge of relief. Halfway and no hue and cry. Lowering his head he put everything he had into the final stretch. He slid under the hitch rail and cat-footed the boardwalk. Then he stopped with his ear against Corrington's wall below the window.

What he heard through that aperture sent a chill through his lean frame. His pursuers had arrived before him. All of them? Eli swept off his hat and assayed a peek over the sill and past a potted plant.

General Corrington stood, tall, lean and imposing, behind his desk. Before him ranged Adam Hearst and his four strapping sons, Matthew, Mark, Luke and

John, while Sally Sue wept from a corner chair. Matthew sported what was rapidly becoming a black eye and one sleeve was nearly torn from his shoulder. The scout ducked, and listened carefully, a plan beginning to formulate.

"General, you have heard my daughter's story from her own lips." Adam Hearst grated. "Your scout toyed mos' cruelly with the affections of an innocent sixteen-year-old chile. Now I want you to order him to marry up with her!"

Air rushed coarsely from Eli's mouth.

"Gentlemen," the general nearly laughed, and Holten took heart. "I'm afraid that's a little above and beyond the call of duty. I can't order anyone to marry."

"Then you and your men best not stand in the way of this family gettin' a holt of this . . . this . . . pervert. I cain't see how a man like that can get in the Army of the United States of America."

"Then why, pray tell, do you wish him for a son-in-law?" The general blurted. Recovering his composure he turned to the girl.

"Sally Sue, are you sure Holten promised to marry you?"

"Why, of course," she piped in all innocence. "Why I'd never allow a man to . . . to know me, in the Biblical sense, if'n we wasn't be-trothed."

"It's just that . . ." Corrington looked heavenward as though to petition the Almighty, though actually speculating on the number of gray hairs his chief scout had added to his considerable stock. Then he rested his chin in the open palm of the hand that held his cigar, to stare straight into the girl's eyes. " Eli Holten goes through women like I go through socks, two at a time."

21

"What a terrible thing to say about *my* Eli!" The girl cried.

"That done it," roared old Adam. "They ain't gonna be no marryin'. They's gonna be a bury'n." He grabbed his wailing daughter and the whole tribe headed for the orderly room door.

As soon as the scout heard old Adam bellowing at the sergeant major he began his scramble through the open window. He'd never have made it if Corrington had not jerked him through by the collar. Unfortunately a plant pot got knocked over and rolled off the sill, outside.

Matthew had already charged through the orderly room and his, "What the hell" came through the window loud and clear. Eli collapsed laughing silently on the floor, unable to rise as he held his sides with both hands.

It was left for Corrington to step to the window with a murmured, "Clumsy of me," And a proper, "Thank you," as the suspicious Matthew handed the cracked pot and broken vine back inside.

General Corrington stood glaring out the window as though lost in thought for quite a while, then ignoring Eli, who was beginning to regain his composure, strode across the office and jerked the door open.

"Sergeant," he bellowed. "Since you seem unable to keep riff-raff out of my office, you will post an armed guard inside your orderly room and another outside guard on the steps. You will do this immediately."

Turning to Holten, the general's eyes blazed, whether with suppressed humor or real anger the scout could not tell.

"*Mister* Holten! It is fortunate for you that you are a civilian employee rather than a member of the United States Army."

By this time Eli had come to his feet. He felt a little

22

hangdog and, definitely off balance; he held his peace.

"Your further good fortune is manifest in the fact that your talent is required elsewhere, providing we can get you out of the fort in one piece, that is."

By this time the blaze had become a definite gleam of humor and Eli breathed a very deep sigh. Too soon.

"Mr. Holten, did you promise to marry that girl?"

"No sir, General."

"Were you aware she was only sixteen?"

"She told me eighteen, sir . . . Uh, I think she did."

"Haruumph." Corrington walked around his desk and sat down. "Doubt it would have made any difference." He grumbled, then pinned Holten with his gaze. "The matter is closed as far as this office is concerned, Mr. Holten. See to it that your romantic escapades stay out of my jurisdiction in the future." The general reached for a memo.

"This came in from outpost number three by telegraph. Their scout reports that friendlies have informed him our old friend, Chief Black Spotted Horse, has been murdered." The general looked closely at Eli's face as he dropped the real hammer. "He was struck down in his own council lodge, not a hand was raised to prevent it, or to stop the murderer from leaving." Eli's jaw sagged and observing this, the general continued. "The perpetrator was a half baked war chief cum medicine man named Wild Dog."

Eli's teeth clicked. "I've met that one, he's aptly named." Then the scout snorted. "Baker's my man at outpost three. I thought better of him but he's been eating loco weed or peyote, maybe both to concoct a story like that."

"You know these Oglala, General. They're not like us, they really believe in their laws; what's more, they enforce them on everyone. No exception." The scout thought a moment.

"Wild Dog is crazy, his name really translates as Mad Dog and he's been apprenticed to old Bad Heart Bull for several years. Bad Heart has, or had a reputation as a sorcerer, I suspect he's dead now. That would be what turned Wild Dog loose."

Eli looked at the commanding officer. "I simply don't believe this."

General Corrington swiveled around and broke out a bottle of good brandy. "I want a direct report by you, on what, if anything, occurred at the camp of Black Spotted Horse." Pouring two healthy snifters, and passing one to Eli, the general then strode to his wall map. "Here is where Baker said the encampment was at the time of the incident. Cheers." Both men sipped the brandy they'd been swirling.

"Your horse, three days rations and extra ammunition are outside the northern sally port. I don't doubt you could best the Hearst family in any kind of a fight but for right now, most of the fort is rooting for them. With that fact in mind, consider the people from the train, and I think you might see the possibility of becoming guest of honor at a necktie party. You'd be amazed at some of the people who feel deeply for the 'plight of Sally Sue'."

"Oh," laughed Eli, raising the brandy to his lips. "Like who?"

"For one," the general took a sip of his drink. "My wife."

First Sergeant Michael Delehanty Morrison of E troop, 12th U.S. Cavalry, tiptoed along the edge of the outer wall and glanced around the corner to make sure the coast was clear. Then he signaled furtively to the shadowy figure that lurked by a water barrel. Eli Holten, chief scout of the 12th, sprinted past the first sergeant and out the sally port where he hugged the outer wall and studied the flat prairie beyond. Chuckling to himself that he finally knew where the little doors got their name.

Satisfied that no hostiles watched, he turned to his Morgan, Sonny, that a blue uniformed trooper held close to the wall near the little-used exit. The scout turned to Corporal Warren Murphy. Eli smiled at the Southerner, a very good soldier who had served as a lt. colonel under Lee. He took the reins of his horse and checked the cinch.

"Ah Eli," the first sergeant began, his bright pink Irish cheeks outdone only by a glaring red nose and thick brogue. "Tis a terrible thing, terrible, when a foin man sich as y'sef mus' flee in shime and shaddas because he dipped 'is wick in a pretty piece 'a pussy! It moikes me wunder what's ta become 'a us all." The Irishman pulled a white handkerchief from his uniform pants and blew mightily.

"It's naut lah'k he's been coaht-mahtialed, Sahge."

Murphy, a lean, wiry figure with a gaunt but strong face that showed the long wear of his career, chided. "He's goin' on a mission. Besides, discretion bein' the better paht 'o valoh."

"More likely discretion to avoid a lynching," Eli laughed as he inventoried his supplies.

"It does seem the honorable thing to do might require you to considah marrying the lady, Suh." The Southerner suggested.

"Shut y'er filthy Johnny Reb trap, Corporal." Morrison growled. "I wouldna' 'spect the likes a' you ta see the tragedy o' dis injoostice."

"Thea's no call foah name-cahlin' . . . ya pooah excuse foah an ovehweight behrel of Ahrish

25

whiskey . . . Cheap Ahrish whiskey et thet!"

"Cheap is it? Cheap! I'll show ya' cheap."

The two men rushed each other, grappled at suspenders and lined up their best shots. Before any blow could fall, Eli grabbed Murphy and swung himself in front of the big bellied, broad shouldered first sergeant.

"Hold it men." Holten boomed authoritatively. "It's bad enough I'm in trouble without you two ending up doing a guardhouse tour. You both have rank to lose—and a drinking habit to support."

Eli's last thought seemed to take effect and both men swallowed their pride.

"Best get back to your duties." Eli finished. "I have to get on with this scout."

"Take care, me bucko." The Irishman boomed in sincere affection.

"Look out foh Wild Dog." Murphy added as Eli swung into the saddle. "Heah tell he spoahts powahful medicine, aside from be'n ootri'ht crazy!"

"Ya'd know a thing'r so about crazy, wouldn'tcha Murph?"

"Don' staht on me Sahge," the corporal warned.

Eli's heels dug into the flanks of his horse, urging him away before he felt called upon to referee another fight.

Johnny Baxter studied the terrain with field glasses from a promontory butte where he and his brother had made camp. Their two prairie wagons formed a break against the wind at the base of the rise. Bobbie Baxter worked a fire to life behind this shelter, using a flint and steel, buffalo chips and a pinch of gunpowder. Johnny was a short but lean man with thin blond hair and sharp, intelligent eyes, though at the moment they were swollen and red. He started down the steep path, doing more sliding than walking and made the last few feet on his butt. Standing up he dusted off his britches and took a swipe at his runny nose with a short cuff then stalked over to the camp.

"Ya see 'em yet?" Bobby asked as he finally got the chips smoldering.

"Hell no!" Johnny cursed. He stomped up to the side of the first wagon and slipped the field glasses into the utility box next to the water barrel.

Bobby looked up from the fire and frowned. He had the same basic features as his brother, blue eyes, although he needed spectacles, their horn-rimmed frame perched on his Baxter-hawk nose, straight, overlarge teeth and thin, light hair. Bobby always leaned to excessive baby fat in the face and middle, he hadn't lost that weight with age.

"You sure this is the place Wild Dog meant?" Bobby pressed.

" 'Course ah'm sure," Johnny shot back. "I talked to him yesterday, Bobby. He said here. The butte with the lone tree south o' Broke Laig Creek."

Bobby looked back to the struggling fire that still flickered weakly. Suffering under his brother's sharp tongue, his mind wandered back to better times.

"Sure wish it were the good ole days, back in Georgia," he sighed.

"What the hell was so damned good about it?" Johnny growled.

"Well ever'thin' befo' the woah," Bobby countered, looking past the fire to the butte with its scraggly oak.

" 'Membah sittin' roun' the Baxtah brewery 'n sippin' suds?"

"So long as it weren't our beer, it was rather pleasant." Johnny conceded. "According to all those friends you so fondly recall, the only reason Sherman didn't burn our brewery to the ground when he came through was he tasted a sample of our product and declared it so bad the South deserved it."

"They was jest put out we didn' die in glorious battle like all those othah idiots," Bobby opined. "Hell we outfitted our hull unit foa the woah, warn't our fault we never made it to the front."

Johnny Baxter smiled to himself. He'd always considered that stroke of genius his saving grace. The Baxter family had equipped a regiment, sure. Hand picked the young men who would serve with it as fellows more interested in making a profit from The War For Southern Independence than dying for it. They'd never been able to muster out to the front, not until it reached them. Then they somehow couldn't locate their uniforms. They'd suffered for all their cleverness though. The Baxter homes had been burned to the ground in spite of the welcoming flags flying from the balcony of their modest thirty room colonial mansion as the conquering blue army marched in.

"It's all yoah fault anyway," Johnny countered. "You can't cook anything worth a shit, let alone brew beer. We should'a sold that brewery as soon as Daddy died, before the war. I always wanted to go into politics." Johnny's eyes glistened a bit with the opportunity lost. "Hell I'd've moved North for a while if I had to. Got me a carpetbag and come back with the Union troops." The older Baxter pondered his calculations carefully.

"Would've been easy ta' become a State Senator . . . Maybe even Governor."

"Remember the good times we had out at the Bristol's plantation?" Bobby continued, showing no enthusiasm for his brother's political aspirations.

"Oh yeah," Johnny bellowed lustily, not minding

28

the interruption of his thoughts by an even more pleasant meditation. "Now you're talkin' some serious pleasure."

They both laughed warmly in the glow of those times.

"Yes sir," Bobby continued. "Ya can't tell me there's anything better than gettin' some o' that nice sweet nigger poontang. Never met a white gal that could take it all like some o' those darkies!"

They cackled happily and slapped their knees with enthusiasm, until something caught Johnny's eye, coming in from the south.

Eli approached the two wagons at a gentle trot. From what he could see the encampment looked as it should, not trying to hide, with tendrils of smoke coming from the cook fire and floating off to the northeast. It looked peaceful and that was what the scout wanted to see.

"Hello the camp!" Eli hollered when he came close enough to be heard.

"I saw you from way out there," the thin man shouted back. "You lookin' for a fire'n maybe some coffee for a noonin?"

Eli smiled. The man spoke gregariously with a southern accent, another good sign.

"Both sound good. I'm Eli Holten, chief scout for the Twelfth Cavalry, out of Fort Rawlins."

"C'mon in."

When Holten stepped off Sonny, final introductions were made.

"My name's Johnny Baxter," the man said, slipping a thumb under a strap of his suspenders. "This here's my little brother, Bobby."

Information was swapped over coffee. The brothers were there to deliver supplies to some settlers who had contracted them to bring food, fodder and

29

ammunition. The scout sought information on the state of the Sioux nation.

"Why, Mr. Holten? Is there trouble out here we ought to know about?"

"Maybe," Eli told them honestly as he accepted a tin plate of cooked antelope the boys had offered him. "We just heard some disturbing things about Black Spotted Horse's camp."

"Black Spotted Horse?" Johnny repeated. "Why his people are camped upstream for the summer. Picked a nice dry spot. Good drainage, and plenty a' water nearby."

Eli nodded. "We heard he was murdered."

Johnny and Bobby exchanged a quick look. It was a practiced deceit they had mastered that could be read as honest confusion and concern.

"Well now, I didn't see the chief himself, ya' unnerstand," Johnny started. "I jest rode up there yesterday. Didn't go into the camp. Ran into a couple a' young bucks, talked a little, ya' know. I saw women and children in the village from across the creek, it all looked pretty peaceful. If it hadn't been we sure as hell wouldn't be here."

Johnny leaned closer to the scout, looking back at his brother, as though for reassurance, then to Eli.

"We're carryin' quite a bit o' guns and the like, for these settlers. Sharps rifles. Wouldn't much care ta' see 'em fall into the wrong hands."

Eli nodded as he chewed on the amazingly poorly prepared meat. The scout's eyes studied the cook, the younger Baxter with the heavier jowls. Bobby smiled a perfect line of white ivory at his guest. Eli smiled back as best he could manage.

"You sure about the women and children?" he asked.

"Well now, that's what I saw." Johnny Baxter blew

into his bandana, then exposed equally white teeth. "Trust me."

The two brothers gave Eli careful directions to the summer camp of Black Spotted Horse. Too polite to tell them he already knew the way, Eli thanked them for the meal and coffee, then headed up the creek.

Johnny Baxter had not dared to use one of his pills with the scout there, although the pain had nearly contorted his face in the middle of the meal. He'd held out for as long as he could. Holten had barely cleared the camp before the Georgian's trembling hands had grappled at the small pouch at his belt wrestled a brownish stained ball from its depth. He thrust the opium into his mouth and swallowed convulsively, then waited for the relief it would bring him.

The moment Bobby saw his brother had regained his composure, he approached Johnny who leaned contemplatively against a wagon.

"Care ta' tell me why we told that bullshit story 'bout that bunch bein' all set an' happy?" Bobby asked his brother.

"Simple enough," Johnny explained in a far-off voice, his eyes glazed and red from the opium. "That man is the chief scout for the only law the Sioux recognize, other than their own. If Wild Dog finishes off Eli Holten, the Army is gonna come out here and do some serious killin'. When that happens, all the guns, ammo and rot gut we can lay hands on will be priceless to Wild Dog."

Bobby smiled at his further revelation of his brother's genius.

Chapter Three

Slowly the sun eased down the sky, headed for its daily death in the west as Eli approached the camp of Black Spotted Horse. The scout felt a warm glow in his heart. The Baxter brothers had rekindled the hope that the general's information might be wrong.

How could a man like Wild Dog kill a warrior as strong and skillful as Black Spotted Horse in his own camp without being fed to the coyotes by the chief's loyal braves? For that matter how could he have killed any Oglala without immediate punishment? Eli simply couldn't picture it, instead he preferred to view the scene as Johnny Baxter had painted it. He looked forward to spending the evening with his brave and noble friend.

When Eli came within sight of the village, several large gaps in the sacred hoop, where tipis had been struck, aroused his curiosity. However a small group of women washing clothes on the creek bank struck a reassuring note. The scout crossed the creek as shadows lengthened and the light turned to a warm and welcome orange. Halfway across Eli recognized a young maiden who had stopped work and boldly watched his approach, a slow smile spread dazzlingly.

"Tall Bear!" she called softly. The other women looked up fearfully at the approaching scout.

"It is good to see the daughter of Gray Otter," returned Eli as he guided Sonny up the bank and dismounted. His mind worked feverishly. Her name is White Doe, he thought, and she's sure become a fine woman since he'd seen her . . . What, two years ago? He walked toward her, carrying his Winchester lightly in his hand.

The beautiful young Oglala's smile faded, to be replaced by a look of desperation, as Eli heard the first pulse of war drums from the circled lodges.

"It is a sad camp you come to, Tall Bear," she started.

"I hear the war drums," Eli answered. "Is it true a great chief is dead?"

The Oglala maid nodded. Tears began to trickle down her round cheeks. "There is no honor left."

"The Oglala know only honor," Eli countered. "Is Wild Dog in this camp?"

Once again White Doe nodded.

"Do not go there, Tall Bear. It is *hmunga*. A mystery to be dreaded."

"I must go to the lodges, I must learn more."

"Then hear my words, Tall Bear," White Doe pleaded. "Five suns ago, Wild Dog rode into this camp with twenty warriors. He killed Black Spotted Horse at his own council, yet so powerful was his medicine, he rode away and no hand was raised to stop him." White Doe paused.

"We were leaderless so council was held; it lasted two days but in the end the band was divided. Eighteen lodges of the Badger society followed Two Ponies to join our cousins the Miniconjou where they will raid the *Hahatonwan;* you say Chippewa, until they feel like men again. Another nine lodges led by Big Buttocks go to our southern friends the Cheyenne seeking their protection. My father Gray Otter wished to make a journey to the *Khay sah pah*. The Black Hills the sacred mountain you call Harney. My father would take the last eleven lodges there as we need spiritual help from this sacred place."

A fresh flow of tears started down the dusky satin of her cheeks.

"This morning, before the order was given to strike camp, Wild Dog returned, this time with ten times ten warriors. My father tried to resist but with only thirteen warriors left it was hopeless. We lost two more braves and my father lies wounded. All were captured, now we are the same as slaves, our men are not allowed to bear arms unless they declare for Wild Dog.

"This morning, after the camp was secured," continued White Doe, " 'Old One-Eye' led most of Wild Dog's men to the east; there are left in camp only three hands of warriors. Most of Wild Dog's followers are not Oglala but *Hohe,* those you call Assiniboine. Outcasts from all the tribes on the plains who banded together in the shining times and took a name for themselves."

During all this narrative, White Doe had kept her head down, as good manners require. Now she glanced into Holten's eyes.

"You are *hunka,* relative-by-choice and I tell you this, if you enter the village, he will try to kill you."

As a professional scout Eli Holten was no fool, though he had grown damned mad. He also quickly grasped the fact that Wild Dog would probably never again be so lightly guarded. Handing Sonny's reins to White Doe, Eli rummaged in his saddle bags for his moccasins.

"White Doe, I am Oglala, I belong to the People and have a name among them. A man has broken the law." Eli sat down and began changing out of his heavy boots. "As a member of the People I must see our laws upheld. If I do not come back the horse is yours, I'll have no further use for him."

Eli walked into the camp hoping he had the mad medicine man doped out correctly. On a horse, fully armed, he would have been too imposing a figure. On foot he did not look nearly so dangerous and could probably shame Wild Dog into accepting his challenge. It was a long chance but those came regularly with the job.

Even without the throb of drums, anyone could tell this was a war camp, the men were in full paint and finery and engaged in such homey pursuits as sharpening blades and straightening arrows. A veteran warrior who was loading .45-70 brass with a Lyman tong tool, put aside his labor and accosted Eli.

"Have you lost your way, white man?"

"I am Tall Bear, son of Two Horns," Eli answered in Lakota. "I come in peace."

"Then go away," the brave shot back. "We come for kill-talks and a war council. Old women and children talk of peace. Which are you?"

Somewhere in the camp voices rose to join the war drums. The scout's heart raced but he knew better than to show it.

"I am an Oglala warrior *Hohe,* stand aside for your betters."

What Eli said was not as suicidal as it might sound, the Assiniboine warrior proved it by getting out of the scout's way. It was one thing for a powerful medicine man to strike down a fellow tribesman, quite another for an outsider to try it. Eli had simply called what he knew to be a bluff.

A paralyzing war cry splintered the air. Eli drew his Remington even before he saw the two braves charge from behind a lodge in the fading light. They hefted war hatchets over their heads, their screaming broke from gaping mouths as they started the bloodthirsty charge.

Eli lined the muzzle up and calmly squeezed the trigger, having automatically cocked the piece on the draw. One hundred and seventy grains of soft lead caught one warrior in his open mouth and blew the back of his head off, spewing gore and watery brain matter onto the lodge behind him. The second brave was not intimidated by the demise of his partner.

He ran headlong at the white enemy, directly into the second round from the big revolver. The slug smacked the murderous brave in his belly, rending and tearing at his intestines. Suddenly the warrior's charge reversed. His legs flew from under him as he heaved backwards. A large chip of bloody vertebrae burst from his back, and he slid another foot after hitting the ground.

A flurry of motion at the corner of his eye jerked Holten around. A stone war club was a blur that would have brained him had he not blocked it with his gun arm. The heavy wooden haft knocked the Remington from his hand and added stars to his vision as it swept off his hat.

A wooden staff slammed violently into the back of the scout's shoulder blade. He fell and rolled, only to see a brave brandishing a hooped stick. Eli's face burned with helpless rage and humiliation when he realized that coup had been counted on him.

Seemingly from nowhere, Wild Dog appeared, an insane light in his eyes, mouth open wide as he chanted his beautiful song. Now Eli could make out the words.

"Hu ihpeya wicayapo! Iwachupi! We shall seize our enemy and smash him about the head and force him to submit to us like a woman."

Wild Dog sang on, describing the death of the white man on all the earth. Eli realized that exactly as Corporal Murphy had said, Wild Dog was insane.

The scout's ten-inch Bowie appeared in his left hand. He sprang to his feet and charged the medicine man. If only he could shove the blade down that vibrating throat, the scout thought, the war would be over before it began. One brave, his bronze muscles rippling with his war cry, stabbed at the scout with a war lance. The stone blade on its tip tore jaggedly through Holten's clothing. Eli yielded to the blade, stepped to the inside of the attack. Too late. The lance slashed a shallow cut under his right armpit. Blood quickly soaked Eli's side.

Desperately the scout thrust at the lance wielder's belly, at the same time maneuvering his attacker between himself and the other two braves. The blade only sank an inch into its target. Instantly Eli slashed at an angle and severed the brave's abdominal wall. Like a gutted buffalo, the warrior's intestines fell to the ground with a wet plop. Steam rose off the warm organs that quivered on the dusty soil. The dying man went to his knees and for a desperate moment tried to stuff his ravaged bowels into his stomach cavity before toppling forward into the mess.

The two other braves leaped their fallen comrade, one wielding a stone war club. The other charged with a tomahawk. They cried out with victory as the wounded scout was thus flanked.

Eli feinted with his knife, suddenly weak from his wound as blood ran into his moccasin. He saw the warrior who had counted coup on him standing nearby, the fact that the man was laughing at Eli's hopeless situation didn't bother him until the brave pulled a knife and leaped to get in on the kill. Anger revived the scout a little, the coup counter had won

37

much honor that day for his deed against the white man; maybe Eli Holten could take the pleasure from it.

Life and usefulness had come back to Eli's right hand. The scout flexed his fist while he slashed once more at the nearest kill. They wre toying with him now and closing in for the kill. Wild Dog rocked nearby, chanting as if far away, his eyes rolled back, lost in his trance.

"Ho! White man," the one who had counted coup on him shouted with a sneer. "When we are done scalping you we shall do as Wild Dog told us. *Iwicahupi!* Even if you are dead, we will fuck you in the ass."

The other two braves snorted in derision. Eli worked slowly to the left. The Remington lay over there somewhere. With the revolver, Holten figured he could at least kill the raving leader of the war band.

A dark shape on the ground behind the coup counter caught his eye. The scout feinted to the right, his three tormentors reacted to the ploy by jerking in that direction. Holten leaped for the small break the move had offered. Three Indian weapons slashed and bludgeoned the air around him. He rolled with his shoulder on the ground, his right hand scooping up the shadowy object. Ending his roll on his knees Eli made a second try at earing back the non-existent hammer as he lined the crooked chunk of wood on the breast of Wild Dog.

For a split second everyone froze, even the mad medicine man faltered in his chant. "Ho! The white man would shoot me with his fire stick?"

The three braves fell back in superstitious awe. Had not Wild Dog changed the big revolver into a harmless piece of wood before their very eyes? In an instant he had done this thing before the entire band. Savage hearts filled with superstitious awe.

A woman's piercing scream shattered the frozen moment, followed by a heavy drum of pounding hooves. White Doe, astride a lunging war pony smashed through the ring of spectators with Sonny half a leap behind.

Eli broke and ran headlong at his horse, vaulted into the saddle, then cut loose with his own war cry as he dug his heels in. The pair smashed into the crowd on the far side. White Doe slashed at grasping hands with the backside of an old cavalry sabre while Sonny cleared his own path with bared teeth.

The howl of cheated warriors broke over them as Eli and the Oglala girl thundered out of camp. Before they hit the creek, White Doe swung close and handed an astonished Eli his Remington. "I nearly got caught," she shouted. "I had to tell Kit Fox I was holding it for Wild Dog."

Once Eli was sure they were out of sight he reined in and changed directions. Walking, the horses could not be heard for any distance and the new moon was not due to rise until well into morning, besides he had no desire to injure either of the horses and he was getting lightheaded. The fugitives rode in silence for several miles before White Doe noticed Eli begin to slump in his saddle. She gigged her horse and took Sonny's reins, pulling in both animals, then dismounted and clambered up behind Eli, whose protests she ignored.

"Tall Bear is wounded," she stated. "We go to a place to treat him."

"I have to get back to the fort." He had to warn the general, the settlers had to be brought in. Everyone must be told that Wild Dog's war path would soon lead him against whites.

"First we hide," she insisted. "Wild Dog is after us. You must rest, then tomorrow . . ."

Holten didn't recall entering the ravine, his mind had been wandering for the last mile or more. Suddenly it was night and he leaned against a low boulder, his butt and legs in sand while White Doe stripped the saddle from Sonny and hobbled both animals. As she worked, White Doe spoke softly.

"I have broken my ties with my people so long as Wild Dog is listened to. There is nothing for me to go back to. I have saved your life and shall care for you now, then you must protect me from Wild Dog. You should kill him."

White Doe walked back towards Eli, traceable only by the starlight she interrupted. Bending down she untied the scout's bedroll from his saddle and spread it beside the scout. She helped him move onto it. Gentle fingers exposed his wound and washed it with water from the canteen. Using boiled moss from a pouch in her own gear she packed the wound, then cut her white doeskin dress for bandages to tie it in place.

There was still a faint tinge of dawn pink on a stray cloud when Eli next opened his eyes. A faint smell of raw liver tantalized his nostrils and he turned to see White Doe rummaging through his saddle bags for salt. A forequarter of antelope lay on its own skin near a tin plate that held the liver and heart. A momentary panic seized Eli, then he saw his bow, still strung and lying across the saddle.

"There's a salt lick at Round Rock. It was too far away so I ambushed the waterhole down the ravine. Antelope eat salt, get thirsty. Your bow too strong, had to get very close." While explaining, she sliced and salted the liver, then fed it to him in long strips.

"You eat all this, I eat heart. Maybe tomorrow we make fire."

Eli slept fitfully for most of the day, sometimes wakening when White Doe clambered down from the rim to rerig shade as the sun moved across the sky. White Doe fed him some more salted, raw antelope that evening and curled up beside him for the night.

By early the next morning, the scout felt good enough to start dreaming. The content of these dreams registered on his blanket which grew a hump in the middle that nearly converted it to a tent. Sight of this little wigwam caused White Doe to jump when she looked sleepily at her patient. Forgetting her restless night she peeled back the blanket. A cry of admiration escaped her, instantly awakening Eli.

Anhe! Hinu! Hinu! She exclaimed in startled admiration.

Eli smiled nervously.

"I have always thought you a brave and handsome man, Tall Bear. But I was never told you could shame a stallion!"

In spite of himself, Eli laughed aloud. The woman's sweet smile belied her warm eyes.

"I do not know if you ever noticed me, Tall Bear." White Doe breathed softly. "But I have always dreamed of having you."

"It was dreaming that got me in this fix." Eli answered lightly as he tried to re-cover his manhood. Their eyes met and the scout felt guilty. He shouldn't have made light of her feelings. He could see the hurt longing in her brown eyes.

The Oglala woman slid down next to her patient. "You know, Tall Bear," she started, stroking the hair on Eli's chest. "There are many ways a woman can heal a man. Liver and potions work best when pre-

41

pared by someone who cares."

Eli ran a rough, weatherbeaten hand gently along the ridge of her jaw, their eyes melted into each other's hearts. White Doe kissed his palm as it slid by. She leaned and kissed the scout's sunburnt neck, square chin and finally her tongue flicked from between her lips to seek contact with his own. The embrace that followed could have softened the hard ground of the ravine with its tender warmth.

"White Doe, pretty thing," Eli cautioned when they broke and the Oglala girl slipped down to his chest. "We've got to get back to Fort Rawlins . . . Warn the Army . . . Warn the settlers . . ."

Eli knew he wasn't dreaming anymore when White Doe slid further down the length of his muscled body to gently squeeze his swollen shaft and work it with both hands, her tongue licking with agonizing slowness at the large head of his organ, her heart racing at the prospect of coupling her ritual beginning suggested. She slipped her mouth over it, a shock of fiery joy shortening her breath. At first she only tongued in circular motions while her small delicate hands slid up and down the phallic pole.

"Course," Eli qualified, waves of tingling pleasure washing from his groin to labor his breath. "We gotta make breakfast, break camp . . ." Longing drove her to engulf all the thick shaft she could as she strove to increase his pleasure.

"Ah hell," Holten cursed. "It is the whole Twelfth Cavalry. If they can't take care of themselves . . ."

White Doe started building the rhythm, faster and faster, sucking harder until Eli thought the maiden would rip him out by the roots. The aching need for release built. Bolts of flashing light and blazing color burned behind the sockets of his eyes until in a creamy gush he exploded into the ultimate.

White Doe whimpered with satisfaction then held him with tiny movements of her tongue, knowing too much would push pleasure into pain. Her perseverance was soon rewarded as the huge organ began to quicken with magical life.

White Doe released Holten with a sigh.

"Damn, White Doe," Eli gasped huskily. "That was good. Mighty good."

White Doe cooed and giggled, then smiled as she slid back to her knees.

"E-li," she bubbled, for the first time using his Christian name, her eyes dreamy. "Not since our great chief was murdered have I truly felt good."

"I know why I feel so good." Eli sighed. "Now why are you so happy?"

"E-li, Tall Bear." She shook her glossy black hair. "Sometimes giving pleasure is all a woman needs." A mischievous smile played around her lips as she undid the leather tie at her throat. "But . . . Maybe not this time."

White Doe's firm young breasts and lightly bronzed skin were set off to perfection by the early morning light as the doeskin dress fell lightly to the ground. Her gracefully formed body narrowed past a firm, flat belly to an exciting flare of hips that framed the enthralling 'V' that culminated in a luscious pubic triangle.

The breathtaking vision of the gentle maiden set fire to Eli's volatile imagination. His semi-rigid shaft began to respond to passion's call, coming to attention, standing straight for inspection.

"Tall Bear," the beauty moaned as she placed one leg on either side of Eli, her lovely cleft inches from impalement by his now throbbing shaft. "Please me. I need you." Her vagina petals were open, pink and dewed with desire, a fiery cauldron awaiting the scout, who like a moth, hungered to be consumed.

Their eyes met, a mutual smile spreading on both faces. She guided the veteran campaigner to the mouth of her oozing, silken purse. White Doe let the tip of Eli's manhood work against her magic peak, egging the panting horse soldier ever closer to the precipice of infinite ecstasy.

All thought of Wild Dog and his madness were forgotten in the heavy, sweet smells of the morning as the two warriors in love met in personal intimate, blissful combat.

"ANHE! Anhe!" She exclaimed as she mercilessly kept Eli from ramming further up her clinging tunnel. "You must rest and let me tend you. Lie back and enjoy." She worked the rubbery head of his huge phallus against her button until Eli thought he would go mad with pleasure. Then with a laugh and a sigh, White Doe's trap suddenly surrounded the rock hard spear and pressed the attack from all sides. Impaling herself, she stifled a shriek of agonized joy as the huge member stretched her nether parts to their limits, then with her man fully encased she let the secret stars wheel in her head, stretching her face heavenward, eyes closed, her mouth wide open as she gasped for breath. Time and space disappeared from her conscious mind.

Eli reached up, seeking her dark nipples, squeezed gently, in hopes he could give as much pleasure as the proud, hot blooded Indian girl gave him. Still she out-maneuvered the soldier with her better mobility.

She began dancing on Eli's spear, thrusting her pelvis down, in circles and back up. She did not fear where the confrontation would take her forces, the advancing white man feared nothing either, he probed every mound, every ravine, every slippery cleft of her ridged and supple terrain. The tempo of battle built for a long, long time. White Doe squelched her ecstatic war cries with each explosion. One, two, three times she clashed against Holten's volleys before he once again approached the edge. Despite the coolness of morning, their bodies grew slick with effort. Every sliding contact of tender, sensitive flesh fired the opposing forces toward oblivion and unrestrained joy. Ever so slowly the pleasure multiplied until their thrilled excitement approached the ultimate assault.

The end came quickly. Eli arched his back, shut his eyes tightly and gritted his teeth as his emplacements were overrun and the beautiful Indian fell to his chest. The walls burst and flooded her with liquid fire arrows of oblivion. Suddenly Eli rolled over on top, seizing the high ground in a lightning counter assault to deliver the *coup de grace,* a smoking fusillade that exhausted his ammunition, he continued with his battering ram until the rigid weapon began to soften and his abdominal muscles gave out. The proud Dakota woman cried out in surrender to the superior forces that showed no mercy. They fell in a heap next to Eli's blanket until their breathing once again had rhythm.

"Oh Tall Bear," White Doe gurgled huskily. "Surely no man can be as great as you."

"We gonna' eat something before we move out?" Eli asked.

"Hmmm," White Doe nodded as she draped a long firm leg over him. "In a little while."

Chapter Four

Holten's trip back to the fort took longer than expected. Wild Dog did not pursue the pair, but White Doe demanded rematch after rematch with the scout. Eli met her in the fields of battle with each request, conquering her each time as the Oglala maiden came to relish the intense emotions of defeat and capture. By the time the fort finally came into view, White Doe had nearly worn her opponent down. The scout felt a sense of relief to be nearing the gate to the compound.

"Must we go in right now?" White Doe asked from behind.

"Lord yes." Holten responded.

Suddenly from outside the walls a large hulking figure came running as if on tiptoes, waving furtively at Eli. First Sergeant Michael Morrison gestured at the scout to follow, anxiously watching the main gate. Eli responded, and turned Sonny toward where the sergeant now ran and put heels to the Morgan's flanks. White Doe sticking like a burr to his horse's tail.

The sergeant stopped at a sally port and pushed it open. Eli jumped off his horse and turned to see White Doe execute an identical, follow-the-leader maneuver. Morrison looked disbelievingly from Eli to

White Doe and back again.

"*Another one,* Mr. Holten?"

Eli gritted his teeth.

"What's the problem, Sergeant?"

"The Hearsts are still here, sir. They're walkin' around the fort, carryin' matched shotguns. Sally Sue has her dress all made. You're goin' to have a right fancy weddin'."

"Weddin'," White Doe repeated the strange English word in confusion. "What is weddin'?" she asked in Lakota.

"It doesn't mean a thing." Eli reassured her in the same language, and patted her cheek, then turned back to the sergeant.

"We can't get the horses through this door."

The good sergeant leaned through the portal.

"Corporal Murphy," he boomed.

The trooper appeared instantly with a pained scowl on his face.

"Ah heah ya' real well Sahgent, no need to holler so."

"What'cha say Murph?" Morrison asked, cupping a hand behind his good ear. "Ya know me hearin' ain't what it was before them fool artillerymen fired the marnin' salute near in me face."

"Ah said—oh!" Murphy raised his voice and continued. "Whut did yuh want me fur Sahge?"

"Take Mr. Holten's mounts in through the main gate. If the Hearsts ask, you found them running loose out here."

Murphy reached for the reins, then his eye fell on the Oglala girl. He looked back at Eli. "Another one, Mr. Holten?"

Eli groaned.

"This is White Doe," he started to explain. "She rescued me from Wild Dog's camp."

47

"Yuh know Mistuh Holten," the corporal offered after a moment's consideration. "Theah's such a thing as bitin' off moah then yuh c'n chew."

White Doe stepped closer to her protector as Eli took her hand and walked her through the entrance, then into a large storage room.

"These Hearsts are a pushy lot." The sergeant volunteered as he led the way. Accordin' ta some a' the people on the train with 'em, they've never had enythin' but troubles with the daughter. Always have, always will. If ye'd stayed out a day'r two more, that accursed wagon train would've left and we'd be done with this foolishness." Eli looked down at the never tiring White Doe and swallowed hard.

"If I'd'a stayed out a day or two more I wouldn't have made it back at all."

"Bad as all that out there is it?" Morrison asked seriously. "So this here Wild Dog is railly on his war path?"

"Yup," Eli answered. "I've got to report to the general."

They came to the door leading into the compound and Morrison forged ahead to check the route. He stepped through it first nearly colliding with Adam Hearst, flanked by his four sons, none of them standing less than six foot tall.

"We-l-l-ll" Morrison greeted warmly, closing the door behind him. "Top a' the marnin ta ya' Sair! Tis truly a foin day fer tha taike'n o' quail."

"We ain't huntin' quail." Old Adam growled. "We jest saw your Corporal Murphy bring in a horse like the one Eli Holten rides."

"One like tha scout roides ya' sie? Well that'd be a Morgan. The general has a couple . . ."

"The saddle was Holten's too," put in Matthew. "We're figurin' Corporal Murphy is helpin' thet no-account get past us."

"Helpin' thet scalawag? Me own Corporal Murphy is it? Why thet dirty Secesh Dee-vil! Surely he'll be punished on accountin' day when tha Good Laird checks our credits 'n debits. Where'd ya' see this shoimeless accessory with the harse?"

"Just now comin' in the gate," John, the youngest Hearst piped. "He wouldn't tell us nothin' though."

"At the gate? This very moment? Why boys. Perhaps the fornicator has na' got inta the compound yit." Morrison pointed to the right of the main gate. "Quick, to the sally port, he'll have ta come through there. It's tha' only way! Hurry lads. I'll stay here and see if he comes through any of these doors! Hurry!"

"C'mon boys!" Father Hearst shouted. Even before they were out of sight, the first sergeant had the door open. Eli and White Doe came out at a run, dashing for sanctuary at Corrington's headquarters.

"Where can I put White Doe so she'll be comfortable?" Eli asked as the Oglala girl matched his sprint like a shadow.

"Why not'cher cabin?" gasped Morrison. "Ye'll sure na be stayin' there yerself."

Falling rapidly behind, the first sergeant finished his thought.

"The Hearsts check yer quarters ev'ry hour, on the hour!"

The general puffed mightily on his cigar, wheeled it to one side of his mouth and spoke from the other.

"So, Black Spotted Horse is dead," he intoned.

"Murdered," Eli qualified with a growl. "And Wild Dog is on the warpath with powerful medicine."

"Humph . . . From what you've just said, you personally helped fortify his position."

"That was fate, General," Eli corrected. "Fate and a freak of timing conspired to make it look as though I'd picked up my Remington, even fooled me a little till I realized White Doe already had my gun and Wild Dog couldn't have changed it to a stick." Eli paused. "He has a song, a long narrative chant that he's claiming contains the death song of every white on the prairie, I'll have White Doe tell this in her own words and translate for you. Perhaps it will help you see the power it has for these people."

It took some cajoling to overcome White Doe's shyness. All Oglala knew that any white man who took the name general was a powerful warrior and must have mystic connections to some long dead hero of the same name. At length, urgency overcame her dread and Corrington heard the maiden's viewpoint.

"Brave men go blind when he speak. They lose their souls to this song of evil. Warriors not separate from song but one with Wild Dog, under his power. Such things are a great mystery and not safe, even to talk about lest the power of this medicine take hold of you and make 'one who follows'."

Corrington was able to follow most of the Lakota words but recognized the value of Eli's translation in such an abstract field.

"I recall talking to Black Spotted Horse at the council fires when we signed the peace treaty," General Corrington reminisced. "A more articulate, noble and honest man you could never find. His speech could have qualified as a song in its own right."

"Perhaps that's why he's dead, General," Eli suggested. "His words may have proven more powerful than the medicine man's song. Shame women are not permitted at council, White Doe can't help there."

A knock sounded at the door.

"Come," the general commanded.

"Sir!" A voice cracked from the opening.

Into the room marched what looked to be a boy of fourteen or so in a lieutenant's uniform. Five foot nine, a hundred fifty pounds, Eli calculated. His short blond hair had been neatly groomed, his posture, arrow straight. He crashed to a noisy but precise halt, stamped through a right face to attention in front of the desk.

"Lieutenant Estillman reporting as ordered, sir!" The young man announced, as he tucked his cap under his arm and rendered an elbow cracking salute to the general.

"You two have met, haven't you?" The general returned the salute, somewhat embarrassed and motioned from Eli to the youth.

"Yes sir!" Estillman answered, his voice cracked like a boy in puberty and his ears flushed scarlet. "Chief of Scouts, Eli Holten, sir!"

"Lieutenant Estillman is commanding 'E' Troop since the untimely demise of Captain Nelson."

The scout remembered now, Jerediah Everett, a settler of the area had become lost in a late blizzard last spring. 'E' troop had gone out to find him. They never did. Instead, Nelson and two men had become separated from the company. The troopers had frozen to death, Nelson nearly so. Later the officer had succumbed to pneumonia. It was now full summer and the Army had yet to send a replacement. Command fell to the junior officer of 'E' troop, to Lieutenant Loren Estillman, fresh out of West Point, at his first post no more than a month when his captain died. It wouldn't be so bad the scout thought, but the kid's voice kept cracking.

"I have an assignment for you Lieutenant," the

general started, setting up three glasses and beginning to pour brandy into each. "And in the interest of its success, and keeping him unmarried and alive, I am sending Mr. Holten along with you."

The Lieutenant gaped at the tall frontiersman, then back at his commanding officer.

"Yes sir!" he barked.

Score one for the kid, Holten thought, he didn't say 'sir, the lieutenant's apologies. I don't understand, sir.'

"Wild Dog, a very powerful medicine man, is on the warpath." Corrington continued. "He's talking death to all whites. I want you to go out and round up as many settlers as possible. You will gather them in a protective column and head them back here. Eli will tell you where and how far to go. Send these people under sufficient escort, then locate and engage the hostiles. I want them pacified."

The general lifted his glass. The lieutenant and Eli followed. Corrington looked coldly at his subordinates.

"Move out at dawn tomorrow. Find Wild Dog gentlemen." He paused, his expression pained, showing the difficulty of his pronouncement. "I've been called a compassionate man, and often a fool by radicals as I am an admirer of the Oglala. Despite that . . . perhaps because of it, I'd not be displeased if Wild Dog failed to survive the battle."

The general swallowed his drink in one tilt of his head. He cleared his throat with a rumble and gusted out a guttural sigh. Then he locked eyes with Holten as the scout and the boy soldier finished their brandy.

"Black Spotted Horse was a friend of mine too. Now go!"

The lieutenant wheeled and marched from the room. Eli guided White Doe by the elbow, then let her through the door first. Memory brought a rueful grin. General Corrington had greeted him and White Doe with the inevitable question; "Another one?" Eli's eye caught that of Corrington's sergeant major, ponderous in size and prestige, the NCO wagged his head.

"Another one, Mr. Holten?"

The eighty-three men of 'E' company fell out three hours before dawn. They spent the time before 'Boots and Saddles' breakfasting, then grooming and preparing their mounts for a preliminary inspection by First Sergeant Morrison whose early morning temper was legendary throughout the 12th Cavalry. In addition to a fully armed trooper, each animal carried a bedroll, saddle, tin cup and pan, canteen and an extra sixty rounds of carbine ammo.

After discussing logistics with Eli and his First Shirt, Lieutenant Estillman requisitioned an additional seven mules; three to carry another sixty rounds per man of .45-70—the regular pack animal would carry pistol rounds—three for rations and fodder and one for water. It gave a total of twelve of the sturdy, cantankerous animals. To insure greater speed and mobility, no wagons would accompany the unit.

"Wha'da'ye call this slop ye've dumped on the back a this good Gov'ment ani'mule!" Boomed the first sergeant, two inches from the ear of a trembling trooper in spanking new blues. "Ya wanna' scatter yer ammo along the trail so yez kin find yer way back? Clean it up! I wanna see that bedroll tight!

Like yer girlfriend's was afore ya' left her to boys back home."

Both lieutenants waited by their horses. To Eli's way of seeing things, they were the only weakness in the troop.

Estillman impatiently studied the men as they went about the task of getting ready. The other officer, Abner Leary, one year younger than Estillman, even fresher from the Point, had been at the fort for only a week. Though far greener than Estillman, he at least looked his age. He busied himself with his own gear and glanced warily at the blustering first sergeant, as though fearing Morrison would soon come over and inspect the officer's packing.

Eli pulled a watch from his breast pocket by its leather fob. Five fifteen. He had time to sneak over to his quarters and see if White Doe had made herself comfortable. The time-conscious Hearsts would not check it again for forty-five minutes.

White Doe fell into his arms the moment he entered the cabin.

"Tall Bear!" she cried. "Five men came. They look for you with big two-shoot guns! They very angry, want kill you I think." White Doe sounded bewildered.

A familiar weight oppressed Eli, he itched to get away from the fort.

"You comfortable?" he asked with evident lack of enthusiasm. "Got what you need?"

The Oglala maiden studied the floor, then cautiously asserted that he was all she required . . . except maybe . . . she burst into silent tears.

"Oh. E-li. There is no fire ring, no hole for the smoke and no sweet evergreen boughs under your sleeping robes. When I tried to cook a meal outside a blue coat came and was rude and made me come back inside."

Eli showed her how to use the stove, open windows and ply a can opener. He'd arranged credit at the Sutler's store in her behalf the previous night so the bed was the only problem still unsolved when the scout headed back to the troop.

Eli found the nervous lieutenants already in the saddle, although the good Sergeant Morrison was not through with his tirade. He'd reached Corporal Murphy and the entire troop waited for his repertoire of biting Irish witticisms to reach a new level.

Eli took the reins of his Morgan as Morrison checked saddle straps and bedding, canteen and carbine. The sergeant huffed and grunted, then with a look of disappointment and admiration, stepped back from Murphy's mount.

"It may be that Johnny Reb outfit lost the war, Murphy, but it sure taught ya how ta soljer." The barrel shaped first soldier turned and began to walk away.

"Compliments, is it? Outta me sergeant?" Murphy jested in a fair imitation of Morrison's brogue.

First Sergeant Michael Morrison froze in mid-stride. A pained expression contorted his features for a moment. Then he turned, a radiant smile illuminating his cherubic face. Much as he liked and respected the black-hearted Protestant Irishman, he was reprieved from having to walk away from Corporal Murphy with a compliment drying in his mouth.

"I heard that! Ya damned unreconstructed rebel, and an Orangeman at that. You wouldn't be inciting yer' poor first sergeant to a fight, would ye?"

Murphy grinned. "Not a'tall, First Sergeant. I only

thought as how ye might be missin' the liltin' sound of the Auld Sod."

Morrison dusted his palms together and flashed Murphy a brief smile, unseen by the other troops. "That's better. Here I thought ye'd be buckin' far some guardhouse time. Carry on, Corporal and maybe . . . just maybe ye can teach these other dumbheads how to care far their outfits."

The broad muzzles of a ten gauge shotgun came to rest on the back of Eli's neck.

"Look what we found boys," Adam Hearst gloated, his four sons still flanking him. "A brother-in-law for ya."

Holten turned, to find the double barrels of Hearst's weapon sticking up his nostrils.

"White Doe got the impression you were going to kill me."

"We were," Matthew answered tightly. "Sally Sue talked us out of it. Are you really paid the same scale as a lieutenant colonel?" There was a hint of avarice in the question.

"Bless her heart," Eli ejaculated with real feeling.

"You want a double ring wedding or just the basics? Choice is yours, since you're payin'," said Adam. "After the trouble you've put us to, that's only fair."

Unnoticed during the byplay, Estillman had ambled his horse over by Adam.

"What seems to be the problem?" he inquired.

"No problem boy," Adam said with a chill smile. "Just making the acquaintance of my new son-in-law."

"Congratulations Mr. Holten," Estillman enthused. "When is the lucky day?"

"Right away, the minute we can get the preacher

here," Luke assured him, his smallpox-scarred features lit by an eager grin.

"I'm not going to marry your daughter, Mr. Hearst," Eli stated, noting that the hammers had not been eared back. Hearst's face, full and muscular, twisted into an ugly mask. His eyes became crazed and more menacing than the twin holes of his shotgun.

"You'll marry my daughter. You're gonna walk under your own power to the church, 'n when the preacher asks you about takin' little Sally Sue as your wife, you're gonna fall all over yourself sayin' 'I do'."

Eli shook his head slowly, never breaking eye contact with old Adam.

"If'n you don't," Hearst growled, a near hysterical note creeping into his voice. "Me and the boys are gonna blow you apart."

Four clicks to destiny sounded loudly over the silent witnesses there on the parade ground as Lieutenant Estillman stuck his Colt revolver in Adam Hearst's ear.

"Don't do that," Estillman requested softly.

A frozen moment slipped by, everyone rigid, but none more statuesque than old Adam, his jaw slack and drooling, eyes wider than any prairie owl's.

"Wha'?" he finally choked out.

"Put the guns down. Carefully please." The quiet command left no room to doubt intent, five men stooped as one and gingerly placed the matched shotguns in the dust of the parade.

"Your business with Mr. Holten must wait," the young officer explained. "We are on an important mission. Innocent lives are at stake and the chief of scouts is vital to the welfare of my command. When we return you are free to take this up with him again, so long as you do not interfere in Army business. Understood?"

Hearst nodded blankly.

"Thank you for your understanding gentlemen," Estillman said coolly, without taking his eyes or gun off the five men. "Sergeant!"

"Sir!"

"Mount the troop," Estillman's command voice cracked only slightly, but retained a hint of ice when he spoke to Eli. "Lead off Mr. Holten."

Eli was already moving when Morrison's bull bellow began the familiar series.

"Prepare to mount . . . mount!"

The eighty-three horse soldiers of 'E' troop swung into saddles.

"Column of two's to the right," Morrison brayed. "Ho!"

The well-trained troopers swung their sturdy mounts to the right and adjusted position to line up in column front.

Estillman touched fingertips to his hat in salute to the passing colors and set spurs to the barrel of his horse. He cantered to join Eli at the head of his troop.

"For-wierd . . . Oooh!" Estillman's voice broke horribly over the command. Somehow no one seemed to notice. They didn't even comment about the furious blush that followed the aural disaster. Most of the off duty officers and men of Fort Rawlins, even the women from soapsuds row, lined up between headquarters and the main gate to see them off.

General Corrington caught Eli's eye with a commiserating glance and the scout couldn't help but grin. Estillman had holstered his Colt before reaching the head of the column. Now he proudly led the way toward the gate. The troop had passed through the main entrance and the color guard returned when a harried *charge of quarters* runner galloped up to the command element. He saluted smartly and handed Estillman a single white envelope. Estillman returned the military courtesy, still smiling a little smugly.

The expression faded from the young man's face as he read the postmark and recognized the perfume. A morose atmosphere settled over him like a cloud.

Chapter Five

"My Dearest Loren," the flowery worded letter began, and that was the last kind thing Deborah Langley, Estillman's betrothed back East, had to say to him. If he truly loved her, he'd resign his commission and become a member of her father's New York brokerage business, or any other occupation in civilization that offered some future, something . . . *respectable*.

The young officer sighed morosely as he finished the letter, refolded it and put it back into the envelope. Her words had revived the long-standing conflict within him.

How he had longed for this commission. His size had made life a struggle. Some bully always figured out a new way to take advantage of him. By the time he had completed eight years of grammar school at the small country primary near his father's large farm and four years at Hubbard Lyceum, he had been involved in twenty-three fist fights and lost all but the last three. Something drove little Loren, though. He struggled with heavy machinery wheels, lifting them over and over until they felt like feathers in his hands. He wrestled pigs and calves from one place to the next, until he could raise a yearling heifer off her feet.

And he hunted.

Every chance he could, the diminutive teenager took an old Kentucky flintlock squirrel rifle, converted to percussion cap, and went out after rare and hard to hit game. He bagged more wild turkey, grouse and lynx than anyone. He read, also, a secret vice unlike that of his friends. Tacitus, Pliny, Caesar, *Lee's Commentaries*. From them he formed a plan for his future.

When he approached his father about West Point, the elder Estillman brayed with laughter. His son's sober countenance calmed him. A senator, whose campaign expenses had always been generously underwritten by the Estillmans, provided the appointment. When Loren reached upper class status, the old man threw a big party. Then Loren had read about the Indians and the West.

A new nation was being gouged out of the unrelenting, but incredibly rich, soil of the prairie. Brave men struggled to make a life in this wild, unforgiving, beautiful place. He wanted to be a part of it. He wanted to protect it and nurture it, and yes, if need be, kill for it. His father tried to dissuade him, but when he was graduated third in his class, Loren chose the cavalry. It crushed his father. He soon learned he had a greater problem.

Deborah and her father didn't share his idea of adventure, this challenge and lure of the country. In Philadelphia, they lived safe, civilized, and in Loren's mind, boring lives in a city dedicated to snobbery. He didn't want it, couldn't live like that. He loved the Army, and despite the freezing cold of the winters and the mercilesly hot summers, he could easily see himself spending the rest of his life in this wild, exciting place.

He loved Deborah, too, though. She had long silky ebon hair that hung to her shapely hips when not wound and tied into a Parisian coiffure. Her green eyes sparkled with wit that could loosen any stuffed shirt, or burn it off with her tongue, depending on her mood and how powerful or important that particular stuffed shirt happened to be. He had courted her with all the guile of a Casanova, the careful strategy of a battle, a conflict he'd been proud to say he'd won by her acceptance of his proposal of marriage. He had sworn to please her, and the Army wasn't her idea of pleasure.

The young soldier's torn emotions got the best of him, ripping and rending his conscious thought with morose exhaustion as he tried to decide what to do.

Eli rode up next to him.

"Come on Lieutentant. We're falling behind."

Estillman looked up to see vast miles stretching ahead.

"Damn," he cursed as he gouged his mount's barrel with blunt Army spurs.

"I wanted to thank you for saving my hide," Eli told the young officer. "You handled that Colt like a regular shootist."

The lieutenant looked absently past the line of horse soldiers.

"First time I ever drew on a man," Estillman said, as if far away.

"Well by my book you couldn't have picked a better time to start."

The mission's first priority was to warn the settlers in the threatened area, round them up and bring them to the safety of the fort. That in itself would be an undertaking, as Eli well knew. He did his best to bring this to Estillman's attention.

"The towns are fairly safe, for now," Eli explained. "It's the small homesteads and way stations that Wild Dog will hit."

Estillman nodded distantly.

"Then we'd best head west of where you last saw the hostiles, round up the settlers on the way back."

The terrain, flat, undulating and monotonous except for occasional ravines and buttes crested with scraggly lodgepole pines, slowly changed to light foresting as they approached the forks of the Cheyenne River. Eli scouted ahead until he found a place where the troops could make camp for the fast-approaching night. So far they had seen no hostiles.

For the first time in many a night, Eli Holten settled down to a long, quiet sleep, no woman to tempt his flesh, no Indians in sight to scalp it and no Hearst boys to blow holes in it. Such slumber can be like a good steak and Eli ate his fill.

Early the next morning, with Estillman's permission, Eli explored far ahead, taking Corporal Murphy and a private along as he checked the campsite he had so recently escaped from.

Morrison stripped the two cavalry horses of their sabres and canteens, anything that banged or jangled that might alert the hostiles of their approach. Still, in Holten's ears, it sounded like a marching brass band as they neared the creek.

They left the horses some distance away from the camp, although the scout suspected Wild Dog had moved out. No smoke rose in the distance, no cooking smells filled the air. Eli left the trooper on the other side of the creek for security, while he and Murphy crossed over, revolvers pulled, carbine and rifle in hand.

As Holten suspected, the band had left, but the camp was not empty.

Four bodies randomly littered the campsite. White Doe's father and his sons were cold and already softened for the long process ahead, although they weren't ripe yet. Still, scavenging animals, coyote and buzzard, had already fed on the easy pickings in the clearing. The fire ring of rocks offered no heat to Eli's probing hand.

Murphy signaled the private to bring the horses, then started to study the terrain in search of any lagging Indians.

White Doe's father and brothers sported several holes, from bullet and lance, though they had not been scalped, a sign of the dishonor in which Wild Dog held them for White Doe's defection. It looked like a hasty execution, Eli thought, recalling the crazed medicine man's taste for torture.

"They must have left within two days after I escaped," Eli speculated aloud.

The private's jaw rested uncomfortably on his bony chest as he stared bug-eyed at the dead men.

"Not a pretty sight, is it?" Murphy drawled. He stepped up next to one of the bodies and peered down.

"No," Private Leo Slocum, a boy from Connecticut, whispered hoarsely.

"No need ta' whisper," the Southerner continued. "You ain't gonna disturb their sleep. This one was Red Moon. I knew him rather well."

"We gonna bury these people?" the private inquired, his face pale. Holten studied the area for a moment before answering him.

"No," he decided. "Wild Dog might decide to send someone back to check the camp. If he does, I want him to find it the way he left it. Besides, their form of buryin' is different from ours. They put the body on a lodgepole scaffold. We haven't time for all that."

"Ya' mean we . . . we're just gonna leave 'em . . . like this?"

Murphy shot him a dirty look. "Y'er new to the

plains, ain'cha, boy?"

Slocum swallowed hard and nodded. "Just joined the Cavalry three months ago."

"Ah, that's right, I remember now. Fresh out of Jefferson Barracks," Murphy answered with a smile that suddenly turned cold and he tersely continued. "Ya' do like y'er told, and you'll live a lot longer out here."

The trooper nodded. Murphy grunted at him and turned to Eli.

"Which way they go, Mr. Holten?"

Eli could only give the general direction. The animals that came to rip and tear at the bodies had obliterated much of the signs he sought in the dirt.

"East," he finally announced. "But we came in that way, so they must have taken a southern path. That's what I'd do. Wild Dog must be heading toward Kadoka, although I'm sure they wouldn't hit anything that big. There's lots of farms in that area, though."

"You sure that's where they're goin'?" Slocum inquired.

"Nope," came the quick answer. Nothing was sure about Indians.

Eli tried to imagine how he'd tell White Doe about her family.

Estillman read his letter for the fourth time that morning, once again falling into his black mood as he dwelled on the lack of understanding of the woman he loved. Murphy and Holten reined in next to him and reported. Eli gave him a detailed picture of the situation. The hostiles were moving east on a southward arc, in his opinion, although he couldn't guarantee they'd continue that way. Estillman nodded distantly.

"We'll swing south, too," he decided as he packed the letter over his heart. "The settlers can be rounded up on the way. If we encounter the enemy, we'll try to attack."

"There's a string of settlements along this pass here, Lieutenant . . ."

"I'm familiar with the area, Mr. Holten," Estillman interrupted, then smiled crookedly. "This is where I got my command."

Samantha Everett struggled with the big copper wash boiler she carried from her soddy and looked sadly across the field where she had planted a small garden. Everything looked wilted and forlorn.

Her husband had plowed the field foolishly in a warm period prior to the last brutal winter. He thought somehow the poorly turned, rock-hard ground would stay frozen in its cultivated state. He'd been so excited by his new piece of property that he couldn't wait for the proper season to prepare furrows for the crops. He'd ruined the plow. Jedediah had such plans for this place, Samantha thought sadly, and when he died, she had inherited the unforgiving land and foolish dreams.

Her own resilient nature would not let her give up, however. She would make it here, with force of will if nothing else. The Oglala came often with fresh game to trade for her meager vegetables, a little coffee and sugar. Sometimes they showed up only to visit. She wondered if the Sioux men courted her in their own way, bringing small gifts of beaded cloth that their wives or sisters had made. But they long ago stopped making any sexual suggestions with their actions, and now doted on her, protected her and looked at her curiously when they thought she could not see them.

Probably wondering what she's doing here,. she thought. She sometimes wondered, too.

Riders appeared from the northwest.

At first she assumed her Sioux friends came to visit, it'd been a while; but these riders rode neatly two abreast, a pennant in the lead.

Cavalry.

The approaching soldiers gave her no sense of comfort, only bitter-sad memories of that recent winter. They never did find her husband's body. He should have known better than to go after that damned stupid mule when it broke out of its corral only an hour before the blizzard hit. It was a useless animal anyway, until they got a new plow. She knew the Cavalry had tried. Trying didn't bring her husband back, though, and now she knew what real loneliness could be for a woman. Then she chided herself for being selfish. Two troopers had died in the search, and that nice young officer.

The column galloped in, passed her soddy and trundled to a halt out next to the corral.

"Troop . . . halt!" the lieutenant shouted. His voice broke every octave. He turned to the first sergeant.

"Have the men dismount," he said softly to Morrison.

"Troop . . . Prepare to dismount . . . !"

Eli studied the woman at the entrance to the soddy. Strands of her hair escaped the tight bun at the top of her head. They hung in her face, tormenting her eyes. Her clothes were clean but faded. She looked old, though Eli knew in the blistering sun of the plains, she might be quite young in years. Her eyes told him, however, she was ancient in her heart.

"Dis—mount!" Morrison bellowed.

"Remember me, Mrs. Everett?" Estillman inquired as he stepped up to the widow and tipped his campaign hat. Eli removed his floppy headgear.

"Yes, Lieutenant . . . Estillman," the woman smiled sadly. "I remember you."

"This is Chief Scout Eli Holten," the young officer started. "Some renegades are kicking up trouble nearby. We're here to round up all the civilians who might be in danger, take them to Fort Rawlins. How soon do you think you can be ready to leave? It's just for a while, 'till we round up the troublemakers."

"The Sioux are my friends, Lieutenant," Samantha answered. "They won't hurt me."

"They aren't just a few spirited Oglala, Mrs. Everett," Eli interjected. "They've got this medicine man from the Asiniboine, and he's packing powerful magic. He killed Black Spotted Horse, Red Moon and Gray Otter. If you're a friend to the Sioux, you know them."

The widow gasped and tugged at her collar. She studied the scout's face for a long time, then pulled her gaze back to the young lieutenant.

"I have a horse, a wagon and a cow. I can leave the chickens behind. They'd only get away if I took them along. If some of your men help me I can be loaded in two hours."

"Too long," Eli advised her. "Make it thirty minutes."

"Really, Mr. Holten . . ."

"He's right," Estillman said gently. He glanced around, looking for his absent fellow officer, and caught sight of a mule in the corral.

"I see you got a new plow animal," Estillman offered.

"No. Same one as before," the widow countered, smiling at the grim joke nature had played. "Old Bud came back after the blizzard was over."

Holten ran out ahead of the column, its ranks swelling quickly with wagons packed with families, cows and pigs trailing behind. He searched for settlements, locating familiar ones, spotting new ones. Some he rode into to tell the hard-dirt farmers, ranchers or trappers about the approaching troopers, others he only took note of. They would lead him too far off his circular route. He would inform Estillman and have riders sent. By that evening, however, every white man in the area knew about Wild Dog, each vulnerable hamlet or isolated soddy aware of the danger. Many of the residents nonetheless opted to stay.

"Ve are der friends of der Sioux," Orsen Brunnen tersely grunted at the scout. He motioned around to the wallowing swine which populated his farm. "Mine pigs and I are as safe as if ve vere on the Rhine! You have to know how to deal vit dem. They are like children!"

"These 'children' want to lift your scalps," Eli answered the German immigrant.

"They are my friends," Brunnen repeated with finality, then returned to slopping his pigs.

Holten located a grassy knoll near a babbling creek for the night's encampment. The wagons formed into a circle, the troopers bivouacking just outside the ring.

Estillman and Leary entered the circled wagons. The troop commander wanted to know how many weapons and how much ammunition the civilians had. Abner Leary looked for a decent meal.

Eli went with Estillman, getting a clear picture of the potential these farmers and ranchers had for defending themselves. Because they had to be prepared to fight off hostiles from their own little sod house, the number and variety of weapons and the amount of ammunition each civilian had surprised even the scout. Together these rugged individualists accounted for a lot of firepower.

"What kind of a war do ya' figure these people intend to start?" Leary asked in a whisper as a trapper proudly arrayed his two shotguns, Spencer repeater, Springfield breech-loader, two Colt revolvers and a Mexican War era musket.

"It's not the war they're going to start," the scout qualified. "It's the one they're going to stop."

"Lieutenant Leary," Estillman started, pondering the trapper's arsenal. "Perhaps you should take charge of organizing the settlers a bit so if we're attacked, they can be of more assistance."

"I'd prefer to stay with the troop, Loren," the junior officer volunteered.

"You will, Leary," his commanding officer answered dourly. "Consider this in excess of assigned duties," Estillman added, using a favorite Army administrative phrase.

Leary scowled as they walked on.

Samantha Everett had her three weapons neatly lined up next to her wagon, a single-barreled shotgun cleaned and oiled, spotless, as were her Remington breech-loader and a .38 Smith and Wesson Baby Russian revolver.

Eli didn't notice the minor arsenal, though. Samantha Everett out-gunned them all.

Her hair, cleaned and fixed in tight flowing curls that cascaded over her shoulders, framed a scrubbed clean face with full pink cheeks and fuller red lips that formed into a dazzling smile. Her eyes twinkled with merriment.

"I clean them almost daily," she proudly boasted. "Not that I get a chance to use them all that often. I hunt a little, but the Sioux have always been so friendly to me . . ."

Eli whipped his hat off, hugged it to his chest.

"Excuse me for saying this, ma'am," the scout began, "but when I saw you this morning . . . well, compared ta' now . . ."

"That was this morning," the suddenly beautiful woman dismissed with a wave of her hand and a smile. "That was before all you menfolk showed up. No reason to get decent when there ain't a man around. Like my dress?"

The simple blue print hugged the widow's hips and breasts, showing off her slim, firm figure. She whirled for the officers and Eli like a flirtatious debutante at her coming-out ball. "It's just . . ." she began, trying to explain her sudden blossoming. ". . . All these people! I don't think anything'll come of this. The Oglala are good people. Wild Dog or not. Even so . . ." Samantha's gaze took in the cluster of settlers, then lingered on Eli Holten. "I'm glad I came. I've been alone for so long."

"To think that such a beautiful creature as you flowers in such a harsh land, Mrs. Everett," Holten remarked, hat still pressed to his chest. "Why, it's enough to make a man an optimist."

"Goodness, Mr. Holten. It seems enough to make a man wax poetic, as well."

Their eyes met, locked together, and Eli felt a quake in his belly that trembled down to his groin. An understanding between them went unspoken, and the scout knew he must prepare a special place tonight, close enough to be safe from Indians, out far enough from the camp to be private.

An extra bedroll laid on top of his between the roots of a cottonwood that overlooked the creek. A canopy of stars winked through the branches and seemed quite special to Eli. He straightened the blankets out, started a small fire, laid back and waited.

The scent of perfume mixed with the scent of

prairie grass cooling in the evening air. Eli looked toward the wagons and saw a lone figure approach, pulling her skirt above her ankles to keep it from dragging on the dirt.

"Hello, Mrs. Everett," the scout offered as the woman drew nearer.

"Hello, Mr. Holten," she responded.

"Lovely night, isn't it?" he continued, feeling somewhat inane as the widow sat down daintily on his blankets.

"Yes, lovely. May I visit?" They smiled at each other like conspirators.

"May I call you Samantha?" Holten appealed.

"Of course, Eli," Samantha answered as she began to undo the buttons of her dress. She pulled the clothing off her shoulders. It gathered at her waist.

Eli reached out slowly and set a work-roughened hand on one of Samantha's firm, swollen mounds. In the light of the fire, he could see the pink nipples hardening from his touch, Samantha sighed softly and smiled. "Do you have any idea how long it's been since a man touched me like that?" Samantha inquired.

Eli moved closer, pulled the woman into his arms. Their first kiss sent a fiery river through Holten's body, gathered in his groin and swelled his manhood.

Samantha's hands sneaked across Eli's chest, undoing buttons, slipping under clothes. She probed his groin and he sucked in air. The widow smiled. Again they kissed, the scout running his hands across her bare back.

"You're all tense," Eli commented as he felt the knotted muscles in her shoulders.

"It's from not having a man," she answered huskily. "Let's see how relaxed you can get me."

Their clothes piled in a heap around the blanket until both of them were naked. Eli slid Samantha to her back, kissed each nipple as he started down the length of her body, kissed her belly, then gently spread her legs and moved his lips toward her swollen mound, covered sparsely by shiny, golden hair. He buried his face between her thighs and Samantha grunted surprise at the emotions that shot through her. She shuddered as his tongue teased the feathery pink lips at the portal of her hot, moistening nest.

"It's been so long," the widow moaned as she ran her hands through Eli's thick, curly hair. He probed and slathered with studied practice and soon brought her to a maddening peak. Her body went rigid and she arched her back as she stifled a scream of joy. The cresting happened three times before Eli pulled back, kissed each inner thigh with a lick of his tongue, then slid the length of her, thrilling at the silken feel of Samantha's flawless skin. The tip of his aching, rock-hard penis probed at the pulsating mouth of her pleasurable purse. Suddenly she tensed and sucked in a deep breath.

Chapter Six

Holten tensed, suspecting danger.

"Don't be a stranger, Eli," Samantha panted.

Ever so gently he began to penetrate the slick inviting tunnel. The woman murmured in his ear and urged him on. The air he breathed seemed full of the aroma of her flesh, perfume and musky-sweet perspiration.

She worked her hips in circles as the pair set a rhythm that shuddered waves of trembling bliss through their bodies. He wedged deeper into her, squeezed by the writhing walls, the gentle friction heating their bodies. Samantha ran her hands along Eli's ribs. The touch of her fingers tortured his nerve endings as he gasped with the passion they shared.

Samantha shuddered, a moan escaped her lips. She buried her face against a shoulder. His own fire stoked toward completion as another spasm rocked her. She held on desperately to Eli as if fearing she would be washed away to oblivion if she let go. The sensations multiplied until their vibrating contentment became unceasing ecstasy. Samantha rode constantly now on the precipice.

The flood waters built and gathered in swirling torrents, until finally the dam burst. Eli gritted his teeth with the out-pouring of his life force. Samantha cried out in surprise.

Spent and vulnerable, the two held on long after, still joined by the golden staff that had made the earth move for her. Finally, they separated. Eli probed her shoulder blades, kneading the knots.

"Your back is still tight," he observed.

Samantha smiled. "We'll have to do something about that."

She slid down his slick body, small hand grasping the spent shaft. Her tongue flicked out, slavered over the sensitive tip of his flaccid member. Instantly it responded, swelled half its length in a mighty surge. Samantha jumped back from its sudden motion, looked up at Eli, shook her head and smiled. Then she went back to working on the thick shaft that promised so much release to the lonely woman.

They started to work on her tensions, first her leg and thigh muscles, kneading the stiff joints, smoothing the tight flesh. Then they labored to soften her back and stomach, exhausting those muscles in a most pleasant way. Finally, only hours before dawn, Eli and Samantha worked out the last tight knot between her shoulder blades. Only then did they sleep contentedly in each other's arms until the sun broke the horizon.

Morning was lazy and, most of all, relaxed for the scout. He rode out early, knowing there were settlements up ahead that he wanted ready to join the troop when they arrived. Speed was of the essence.

Suddenly the scout saw a smoke smudge in the clear blue sky ahead. He rode warily toward it.

A small rise gave Eli a point of observation. He left his horse below the crest of the hill, walked up to the ridge. He used his field glasses to look down onto a flaming barn and smoldering soddy.

Bodies, four of them, lay scattered in the clearing around the burning buildings. No hostiles in sight.

The sound of hoofbeats made Eli glance over his shoulder. Corporal Murphy galloped up, jumped off his horse before it had come to a full halt next to Eli's Morgan and pulled out his Springfield carbine. He ran up to where the scout lay prone, peered over the edge.

"The lieutenant saw the smoke," Murphy explained. "He sent me ta' find you."

"Ride back," Eli ordered. "Tell him to put the wagons in a circle, then run the troop up here. Wild Dog can't be far."

Warren Murphy's horse foamed with exertion as he reined up next to Lt. Estillman. The relief force had halted, with extra out-riders on all flanks. The kid lieutenant made a good soldier, Murphy thought appreciatively.

"Mr. Holten's lookin' at a burnin' soddy over yonder, sir," the Southerner reported. "He says ta get the wagons in a circle and high-tail the troop over th'ar."

"But . . . that would be splitting our forces," Leary protested. "Like Custer at the Little Big Horn."

The women in nearby wagons audibly sucked in their breaths.

"Must you speak so loud, Lieutenant Leary?" Estillman snarled. He looked back over his shoulder at the wagons.

"Most of them have better firepower than we do. Besides, our orders were to engage and pacify the hostiles. Put the wagons in a circle. Sergeant Morrison!"

The troop came charging down the rise to the collapsed remains of the soddy, only smoldering now, having burnt through the wooden ceiling beams. They found Eli standing over one of the bodies.

The two older people, a man in his thirties, a woman in her mid-twenties, had numerous arrows in them. The two small boys, ages around six and ten, had been bludgeoned to death. All four bodies had been hacked at, mutilated, bloody scalp locks freed from the rest of their hair.

"We're too late," Estillman said the obvious.

"They rode east," Eli replied.

"They could be drawing us further away from the wagons," Leary feared.

Eli had been staring long and hard at the eastern horizon, now he pointed at the beginning smudge of a black plume, southeast of their position.

"There they are," he announced.

"We have to hurry," Estillman exclaimed. "E Troop! Move out!" Eli winced at each fractured syllable the young soldier's voice cracked on.

The scout's great Morgan ran far ahead of the charging troop, up a slow rise to a clump of cottonwoods that clung tenaciously to the edge of a butte. The homestead, which flames still struggled to engulf, sat two hundred yards below. Eli could hear the screams of Wild Dog's victims.

A score of painted warriors yipped and howled as they ran about the farm, some still dashing in and out of the soddy, although the flames already danced out the windows and licked at the roof supports. Movement to one side attracted his attention.

A man, arrows in his shoulder and thigh, struggled loudly as four braves dragged him to a stout tree near the corral. They began lashing him to the trunk, twisting the arrows in him. He howled in mortal

77

agony, but not with the same horror as when another group of savages, who wandered around one side of the soddy suddenly fell on the earth and tore up a piece of it.

From the depths of a carefully prepared hiding hole, the Indians hauled out a young auburn-haired woman. The renegades yipped and hooted in triumph as they dragged the terrified wife from her refuge.

"No!" the man screamed, oblivious of the sticks and twigs the Indians had built at his feet. "Leave her alone. Please . . . don't hurt her."

"Luther!" the woman cried. The red men ripped her clothes off.

"Jenny . . . Jenny, I love you," Luther cried as the marauders set fire to his feet.

Eli scooted back from the crest, ran to his horse. He mounted it in one leap, then rode full gallop for the approaching troopers. At the sight of the thin plume of dust, Estillman began to rein his horse back and gave the command to halt.

"Don't stop on my account," Eli shouted as he whirled his horse around. "Take a little cut around this rise and you'll land right on top of 'em."

"How many?" Leary asked nervously.

"Enough for everyone," Eli answered. "Hurry. There's some settlers there still alive."

Again the Morgan pulled Eli out ahead. He motioned for the lieutenant to go around the rise, while he dashed up it, this time to the ridge. He pulled his Winchester free of its scabbard and reconnoitered.

Flames engulfed the screaming man named Luther. His clothes peeled off with his boiling flesh as he howled. Nearby, the woman called Jenny lay pinned to the dusty ground as four braves lustily raped her. One warrior hooted with completion, his reddened penis thumping into the woman's dry receptacle. He pulled out for the next man to take his turn. She struggled to escape him and the warrior's open palm smacked hard against her face, knocking her senseless.

Eli brought the roan-covered Morgan to a steady halt. He put the Winchester to his shoulder, sighted in on the warrior with the big palm.

When the Winchester cracked, the braves below froze or turned to look, except for the one on Jenny's chest, who emitted a shower of blood from his shattered head, leaped and rolled over the top of the prone woman.

The Cavalry came howling in around the rise. The golden notes of the charge sounded crisp in the smoky air. Eli charged down the slope, chambering another round in his repeater.

Shots cracked from both sides as the hostiles ran for their horses. The Cavalry peeled into a 'V' and raced headlong through a plowed field. The scout came in close from a right angle.

One of the four raping warriors, his hardened spear still sticking out from under his breechcloth, picked his war lance up and caught a trooper in the shoulder as the troop wheeled into the farmyard. The lance spun the soldier off his horse. He fell heavily, bleeding onto the soil.

Sonny carried Eli through the bedlam of the assault. From a near gallop, the scout aimed and fired at the brave. A chancy shot, but the lustful warrior leaped skyward and did a mid-air dance, twisted and writhed from the impact of the .44 slug that caught him below the left nipple, his heart already burst from the hydrostatic shock.

With a whirl of the Winchester, Eli chambered another round, took aim at a warrior already half-way into his saddle and fired into the brave's back. A red-rimmed black hole appeared between the renegade's shoulder blades near the spine. The slug exited below the Indian's throat, bringing forth a flowering scarlet plume. The impact catapulted the body over the horse.

The warriors who managed to get to their ponies scattered in all directions, cavalrymen in hot pursuit.

"Stay together, me buckos," Morrison cried out. "Don't go wanderin' off so those red savages can play wit'ya at their leisure."

Jenny, tattered clothes hanging from her violated body, desperately threw sand on her flaming husband's form, tears spilling liberally down her face. "Somebody," she wailed. "Help me."

Eli slid off his horse, his Bowie knife pulled. With a quick slash he cut the rawhide thong that held the settler's body against the scorched tree. Luther fell free with a spill of fluids and Jenny wailed anew.

Lieutenant Estillman leaned over to Leary.

"Throw something over her and take care of the poor woman. We better get back to the wagons." The young officer turned away, looking around. "First Sergeant!"

Morrison came running.

"Two wounded, sir. None so bad that they can't fight again," the Irishman reported. "And we killed six of those red dee'vils."

"There's plenty more where they came from," Eli called out as Leary covered the settler's wife with a blanket and led her away. Eli stepped closer to Estillman's horse. "The man's dead. Not much we can do but bury him."

"You heard the man," Sergeant," Estillman intoned in a tired voice.

Wild Dog's song pounded on in his head, a never-ending chant that he babbled now under his breath as he studied the sticky, syrup-oozing, brown-stained ball in his hand. He smiled when he thought of how it intensified his song so he could go dream-walking at will. Before he did that, though, he must speak to his growing throng of fellow singers, the warrior-followers of his powerful medicine.

He stepped toward a large boulder that sat in the clump of pines where a portion of his band had made camp. Soon the raiding party would be back with more scalps and white man's horses. Now was the time to build the others up for a big fight.

"Hear me, warriors," he cried out, his death-rictus grin pulling at the corners of his mouth. "I have had a vision!" he shouted. "In that vision I see that the pony soldiers gathered the white devils together to lead them to the great lodge where they hide behind walls made of trees. In my vision, I see many warriors with many scalps on their belts, all riding as one with the song. I see burning white lodges and white women at these warriors' feet. It will soon be dusk. If we ride fast, we can strike the pony soldiers tonight, kill many of them before they can escape to their fort. Soon we will be great enough in numbers to overwhelm even that place.

"First, you must make the song part of you, until it plays in your minds always like it does in mine. I hear many of you chanting at night. That is good. Only you must always sing the words I have taught you. You must sing until there is nothing else in your minds. For now, you must mount and ride, for tonight we raid the white-eyes and their pony soldiers, to let them know nothing can protect them from my medicine!"

81

The caravan slowed with each new wagon that swelled its number. With the news of homesteads being burned, the whites of the region sought E Troop out. By Eli's recollection, they were still one day out from Fort Rawlins.

The relief force made camp on a wide sandy shelf that overlooked a narrow strip of water that had banks wide and high enough to hold a mighty river. Eli scouted the tall reeds and saw grass around the camp to make sure none of Wild Dog's band skulked too close. The settlers turned grim with the stories of the two farms that had been burned and the people killed.

"What's the Army gonna do about this?" one irate citizen blurted out at Lt. Leary.

"Gee, I don't know," the green second lieutenant offered defensively. "I just got here."

Morrison stationed pickets around the perimeters of the camp even before the evening meal started being cooked. Eli entered the camp before dusk began to take its toll on the light of day.

"What's it look like?" Estillman inquired.

"We're being watched, but that's to be expected. We have to make some time tomorrow, though."

Estillman nodded and squinted toward the east. "Just let it be a quiet night," he prayed. "That's all I ask."

A flaming arrow whipped through the air and thocked into the side of a wagon. A woman screamed.

"E Troop!" Estillman shouted. "Prepare to engage hostiles!"

The horses, mules and wagon animals had already been hauled inside the circle when a flood of screaming warriors descended on the relief force. In the failing light the troopers and settlers began a fusillade that belched white plumes of gritty smoke at charging braves who burst down upon the defenders. The twilight turned red-orange with muzzle blasts.

A howling Wild Dog jumped his horse over a wagon tongue and ran through the milling circle of defenders before he vaulted out the other side, unscathed. Children cried as mothers held their infants to their bosom. The air became thick and fouled with the clinging smoke from gunfire. Flaming arrows smacked into canvas wagons, war lances thumped into the ground. Horses panicked in the circle. Lead bit into wood, digging out splinters that shot in every direction. Bedlam became a place of calm and quiet repose by comparison.

Estillman stood near the back of a wagon, staring coldly at the charging Indians as though trying to see their souls. A warrior howled his ear-splitting war cry and charged the lieutenant, his lance positioned to run the white man through. Estillman coolly raised his Colt and fired into the chest of the brave's horse.

With a yelp of surprise, the red man catapulted over his mount's head and crashed down against the side of a covered wagon. Eli leaned out and shot the attacker in the side of his head. The bullet deflected off his spine and raced downward, shredding his larynx, right lung and came at last to rest in his liver. Blood gushed from the dead man's mouth.

With the speed of its sudden start, the intense battle came to a halt. Wild Dog's braves ran yipping off, firing random shots over their shoulders at the wagons. Two of them hauled a milk cow and shooed some pigs in their way. The silence that followed rang in the ears of the beleaguered settlers and troopers, until crickets began to fill the gloom with rhythmic chirping and a bullfrog started his evening chorus.

"Casualties?" Estillman inquired calmly.

"Four civilians wounded, sir," the first sergeant

rumbled. "We lost two cows, three horses and four pigs to those heathens."

Estillman nodded. "They'll eat well, won't they, Sergeant?" Then he turned to the scout. "What was all that about, Mr. Holten?"

The scout stared after the attackers. "I don't know. But you can bet it made sense to Wild Dog."

"Now do you see the power of my medicine?" Wild Dog howled as the warriors, consumed with the thrill of battle, danced and chanted, the magic song still racing in their blood. The outcast knew his catch looked puny, a few cows, some horses that broke loose, the sweet meat animals, but the song told him it meant more. That night, the crazed medicine man took the last two opium pills he had, then went dream-walking.

Eli searched the camp as the settlers stamped fires out with blankets and shovels. Horses were rounded up and at the insistence of the settlers, the troopers camped inside the wagon circle. The crowded conditions made it hard for the scout to find her, but finally he stepped up next to Samantha as she settled her mule down for the night. The widow looked startled as he took her hand, then relief flooded into her face.

"Oh, Eli," she exclaimed. "You're all right."

"I see you're fine, too," Eli answered.

A trooper stumbled into Eli's back.

"Sorry," the soldier mumbled over his shoulder.

"More than a little crowded here tonight," Samantha commented. Eli smiled at the lovely widow.

"Would you like to go somewhere that isn't so . . . busy?"

Samantha coyly smiled. "Where?" Then alarm filled her eyes. "Not . . . outside the wagons," she gasped. "What about the Indians?"

"They're gone for now. Besides, don'cha think I can protect you?"

To Samantha's surprise, the spot they slipped away to, like a pair of young lovers, had a sentry posted right above it. A small backwash with an undercut bank, it formed a part of the wide, sandy flat of what had once been the bed of the great river out of sight of any curious folks from the wagons. The trooper winked knowingly as Eli tried to explain why he wanted the soldier posted there to fire a warning shot in the event of trouble.

"I think I can do that for ya, Mr. Holten. Another one, huh?" The soldier grinned.

Samantha showed a new side to herself that evening. The night before, she'd been like a young yearling colt, full of life and explosive energy. This night, in the tall waving grass, after the initial rush of ecstasy, she went to all fours and settled down to a plodding love-making. She had the stamina of a plow-horse, doggedly leading Eli to the fringes of her fields, his ample stalk the plowshare, turning the rich soil of their passions as Eli dug the furrows deeper.

Her thews, once tense and tight, were bands of strength from hard work and a harder life. Holten could not imagine, though, how she developed the writhing muscles that pulled at his staff so mightily in the fits of satiation that seemed to wrack her body, her ample firm breasts swaying as she worked her hips with such vigor.

This time they fell exhausted after only a few hours. Last night had been to make up for a long, cold winter and a longer spring. Tonight was just for tonight, and now sated, she dug into the crook of his arm, breathing softly.

In the rosy afterglow, Eli counted stars, his mind on other things. Unbidden, a thought jumped into his consciousness.

He wondered what happened to the Baxter boys. They had told him they'd been to Black Spotted Horse's camp, that everything had been fine there. Had they lied? Or had they been there before Wild Dog? Why, he reasoned, would they lie about something like that? Were they safe now? He recalled the meal they had fed him. He'd never encountered an honest piece of fresh meat that tasted so bad. If they fought like they cooked, Eli had very little confidence in their ability to survive Wild Dog.

Samantha's stirrings interrupted his train of thought. She murmured soothing words and urged him to another bout of plowing. This time when they finished, Samantha asked Eli to walk her back to her wagon. They dressed and headed toward the circle.

The guard winked knowingly at Holten as the couple walked by.

"You're not mad at me, are ya', Samantha?" Eli queried.

"Heavens, no," she answered. "I just have to get some sleep, and if you're nearby, that's not going to happen. As it is I'm going to spend the night dreamin' about you.

"Besides," she continued with a wave of her hand, "there's always tomorrow."

"We'll be at the fort tomorrow night," Eli protested.

"Fine," she answered. "We'll find out if you're as good in a bed as you are on the ground. What do you have, cabin or what?"

Eli felt a bolt of metal ram up his spine and he came to attention with a jerk.

Good Lord, he thought. I got White Doe in the

cabin, Sally Sue outside. So where could he put
Samantha?

"Cabin," he answered her and his voice cracked like
the lieutenant's.

Chapter Seven

Wild Dog and a dozen braves howled into the Baxter camp at sunrise. Both boys smiled in unison and the deep crimson sun reflected off their tombstone-sized teeth, making it look like they had mouths full of blood. They were glad to finally get the crazy savage to their wagons. They'd been wandering around for three days trying to locate him after their last contact outside Black Spotted Horse's camp.

"I have come for rifles and *whis-bah!*" Wild Dog shouted as he leapt off his mount. He ran up to Johnny and the medicine man's smile trembled from ear to ear as his eyes gleamed far back in his head.

"But most of all," he continued to the white trader, hands starting to tremble. "I have come for the dream-walking pills."

Johnny winked knowingly at the medicine man.

"Ah call 'em stomach medicine, myself," he confided. Then he pulled a single brown ball of opium from his pouch. He raised it to eye level, both he and the savage studied the sticky tan ball of ecstasy. Wild Dog drooled. The moment he reached for it, Johnny popped it into his own mouth.

"Now," he said after he'd swallowed the pill. "What do ya offer me for the guns and firewater that I done brung ya?"

Wild Dog lost his smile.

"Your lives," the medicine man answered back evenly.

"Here," Johnny countered, pulling at his opium pouch. "Have one for yourself. No, take two. They're small."

Wild Dog studied each ball avidly as his nervous grin returned. Then he snorted his approval and swallowed each ball. His eyes narrowed and he stared at the trader.

"Do not think I am fooled by your white skin," the madman ranted just above a whisper. "I know you are just shadow people. If you weren't, I would kill you right now."

Johnny forced a nervous smile back on his face. "Right," he agreed. "Just happy-go-lucky shadow people, lookin' ta make a dollah. Now . . . er, what about th-the guns and the firewater?"

"And the dream pills," Wild Dog added. He pulled a large stuffed leather pouch from his scalp belt, opened its draw strings and turned it upside down. Out poured gold and silver coin.

The other braves restlessly watched the transaction as Johnny bent down before their leader and began scooping up the money.

"More," Johnny demanded from the ground. "I want more like this."

Several of the braves snickered in contempt. Of what use was this shiny metal? It was too soft to make good arrow points and too small to wear around the neck like the Washington medals.

Wild Dog turned back toward One-Eye, who jerked another stuffed pouch from his belt and threw it to Wild Dog. The medicine man dropped it where the Baxter boy struggled on the ground.

"We attack many dirt hole lodges where the whites

hide. We kill many whites, take many women. You tell us to look for this shiny metal in clothing and the wood boxes that pull apart. We have many things that you told us to look for. Is this enough?"

"More," Johnny's greed declared. "At least three more like this." He raised the last pouch thrown to him.

"Why do we not kill you and take what we want?" One-Eye shouted from where the other braves waited.

"Because then there'd be no one to bring the dream-walking pills," Johnny yelled back. He gave Wild Dog a sly smile. Wild Dog licked his lips nervously, thinking about the possibility of no more quick trips to the dream world. The two balls of opium he'd swallowed hadn't begun to work yet. His mind still functioned in jagged clarity. No trips, no visions, very quickly, no power.

The equivalent of three more pouches dropped to the ground in front of Johnny Baxter, including silver picture frames, gold watches, wedding rings and gold fillings.

"You remembered about the teeth!" Bobby yipped gleefully.

"Good boy," Johnny told Wild Dog. "And just to show our great good faith, we brung ya a present." He signaled Bobby, who crawled onto the seat of the rear wagon.

He lifted the canvas that covered its bed and dragged a small white girl out from under it. Her eyes darted fearfully around, not understanding. The thirteen-year-old's wide-set eyes drooping mouth and slack features betrayed her limited wit, but did not stop the warriors from reaching for their loincloths with lusty enthusiasm. She did, in fact, have a sweet smile, lovely blonde hair and a newly developing body, despite the mental weakness.

"For only the price of a buffalo robe, this fine piece of white feminine fluff is yours for the fucking!" Johnny hawked. The price fell at his feet.

One-Eye trotted his horse up next to the wagon and grabbed the girl by the crotch through the thin fabric of her dress.

"Hi, Mister," the girl simpered. "Will you be mah friend?"

With a grunt of impatient lust, One-Eye jerked her to his horse. She squealed with delight when she felt his stiffened member as he took her to a corner of the camp.

Immediately the other braves got into the wagons and hauled out the rot-gut whiskey, the Spencer repeaters forgotten for the moment as the revelry with the retarded girl mounted. Whoops of excitement blended with her joyful shouts. They tore at the corks and swallowed fire for their bellies to match that burning in their loins.

"The dream-walking pills," Wild Dog begged.

"They're extra, ya know," Johnny noted with a forced smile. His eyes had become redder and his nose itched to run.

"You have taken all the shiny metal," Wild Dog protested. "There is nothing left."

Johnny studied the five bags of gold and silver and the ornaments he'd set up on the first wagon's seat. The profit margin for this transaction exceeded two hundred per cent, including the opium. Besides, if he didn't give the medicine man the pills, Wild Dog would kill him and get them anyway. The Baxter boy smiled magnanimously.

"Well, since we're friends," he intoned hypocritically. He pulled the opium pouch from his leather belt and gave it to the warrior.

Wild Dog made a high-pitched moan as he

accepted the pouch. Then he smiled eagerly and looked to where the simple-minded child lay prone, her skirt up around her neck, legs widely spread. The mad savage hooted and dashed to join his fellow warriors.

One-Eye came walking up, adjusting his loincloth, a smile of satisfaction on his face.

"Show me the rifles you have brought us," he demanded.

"They're right up here," Johnny pointed over his shoulder to the wagon he sat upon. "And, One-Eye, I got an extra special present for you."

Wild Dog's second in command looked suspiciously at the white trader, the smallpox marks on his ravaged face looking like white freckles. "What present do you give me?"

"Ten wagons," Johnny answered, smiling. "You'd have ta ride hard and fast but it's where I stole . . . er, found that purty little thing you boys are jumpin' on. I just happen ta know they don't have all that much ammunition, and they got some really fine white girls for you to play with. A little older than this one, with big tits, tight little asses . . ."

Johnny Baxter gave detailed directions to the wagon train he and his brother had seen two days earlier. One-Eye grabbed his horse and yelled to his own band of men.

Bobby walked over to his brother. "Ah thought it went purty well, didn't you?"

"Shut up, Bobby," Johnny spat back. He turned to the utility box, pushed his field glasses aside and dug deeply into the wooden container until he found a large tin box. He couldn't decipher the funny looking Chinese writing on the outside, he only knew that it held what he desperately needed right then.

With quaking hands and gasping breath he

struggled to open the sealed container. The nearness of his relief weakened him. Finally he wrestled out two brown balls and stuffed them into his mouth.

One wasn't enough anymore. Two barely let him hold his ground. It took three now to make him feel good. Johnny swallowed hard and waited for his own dream-walking.

Two Ponies lifted the pipe, releasing large puffs of smoke to the spirits of the East, South, West, and North, to the sky and to the earth, then sucked on the mouthpiece again until the rich taste of tobacco and *knickanic* filled his lungs. He prayed for the goodness of the taste in his mouth to be an omen, that he might find an answer for his brothers tonight. He held the pipe in front of him. Everyone in the lodge had now smoked. The gathered members of the *Ihoka* society waited for Two Ponies to speak.

He turned around the circle to let everyone know he would begin and a silver amulet with a bas-relief of George Washington hanging around his neck twinkled in the firelight.

"My brothers of the *Ihoka*," he began. A black stove-pipe hat sat straight up on his head. His fellow initiates of the Badger warrior society waited patiently, knowing their war chief would tell them what was on his mind at the right time. The proud face of Two Ponies again turned to each of his fellow warriors, who circled the ring of stones before he continued.

"I have called you here," he began in a rumbling voice that every man in the lodge could hear, "to talk war. What I ask you to tell me is, who should we make war with?" As though chipped from red pipestone, his countenance held a noble cast, lit by the dancing flames they sat around.

A rumble of curious grunts went up. Several of the warriors crossed their arms and considered the question carefully.

"We were all there when Black Spotted Horse was killed by Wild Dog. We will not speak of this tonight. I hear that my friends, Gray Otter, Red Moon and Wounded Elk are dead, killed in their own camp," Two Ponies boomed. "I hear that again Wild Dog, that outcast of the Oglala who rides with the Asiniboine, has done this. Now I have been called to join Wild Dog on the warpath against the white-eyes, although that person has broken our laws. Council me, brothers. Who should we make war with? Wild Dog . . . or the white man?"

Mutters of consternation rose. An older warrior, respectfully called Grandfather by his brothers rose, reached for the pipe, cleared his throat and spoke.

"There are two here that were present, Two Ponies, when Gray Otter and his sons died. Perhaps we should ask them to tell us what happened?" The old man gestured politely with his chin toward two young braves. One softly chanted as he sat crosslegged. He was the first to stand. He rudely ripped the pipe from the old man's hands and began to speak.

"I am Small Eagle. Like all of you, I was there when Wild Dog sang his song," the warrior started. "Some of us gained much power from it. When Wild Dog sent Black Spotted Horse off to the spirit world, many among us did not approve of this. Lodges were taken down and many left. You among them," he sneered at Two Ponies. "Gray Otter, Red Moon and Wounded Elk also did not like the song of Wild Dog. Only they stayed behind and spoke bad words about Wild Dog. Even so, he would have spared them. But when a white man came to the camp and attacked Wild Dog,

Gray Otter's daughter came to his aid. Wild Dog's medicine had turned the white man's revolver to a stick. He was helpless until White Doe rushed in with horses and they rode away.

"After that, Wild Dog went to speak with Gray Otter about this. But that person wanted to fight. Even though he raised his hands to defend himself, like a strong wind, Wild Dog washed over him and ripped at him. Gray Otter's sons then unfairly attacked Wild Dog." Small Eagle's face, dulled by Wild Dog's song, filled with awe as he continued to recount his version of the story. "Wild Dog fought like smoke! He passed around and through these three bad people. His medicine had more power than all of theirs. His medicine is greater than all the white man's guns and numbers." The young brave pointed with his chin at the gathered warriors. "You should join Wild Dog as I have. Learn his song so that we might all rid our land of the white men. Small Eagle has spoken."

The other young brave rose to his feet, studied Wild Dog's creature with disdain, then took the pipe and turned to Two Ponies.

"I am Buffalo Udder. Like all of you I saw that person Black Spotted Horse. Now his skulking dog comes and speaks to us of this mighty song. That song has twisted that person's tongue. The white man was not a white man, but an Oglala. It was Tall Bear, whose eyes work for the pony soldiers. He came into camp on foot. Wild Dog would not fight him. He hung back and sent others to do this for him. Some people were killed and wounded and still Tall Bear had not been badly hurt. He grabbed up a stick lying on the ground, thinking it to be his gun. At that time White Doe came with Tall Bear's horse and he mounted. They rode away. Wild Dog was very angry at this. After that, Wild Dog sent some men, under

One-Eye to kill Gray Otter in his sleep. When his sons heard their father being murdered, they came to his aid. They fought bravely, but there were too many of Wild Dog's followers. All three died. We were all there when Wild Dog leapt to his feet during a council and killed our leader. Now he orders the deaths of others. I have no love for the white men. You all know that. Yet, I say we join them to seek vengeance for the murder of our brothers."

"No!" Small Eagle cried out. "Wild Dog has the medicine! He has the power!"

"I do not deny his medicine is mighty," Two Ponies interjected after he rose and gently took the pipe from Buffalo Udder, to emphasize Small Eagle's rudeness. "But I remember that Wild Dog's name is not his own. He was once called Dog Running. He was renamed after the dog that has foam in its mouth because of a fearsome and uncontrolled temper he had even as a small boy. It is told that his whole family had always been afflicted with this sickness. Whenever any of them fell to the ground and foamed at the mouth, they would later go and do evil things. That is why they were cast out of our tribe many, many summers ago. Only then did they join the Asiniboine, the cast-outs of all other tribes."

"It is not sickness, but visions that possess Wild Dog," Small Eagle insisted. "His strength is that of the buffalo. Nothing can resist him. Nothing can stop him."

"He killed four of our tribe," Buffalo Udder countered. "If Wild Dog is powerful but evil, should we not resist this evil? Should we join him only because he is powerful? He has broken the law. He should have been struck down when he murdered Black Spotted Horse. We should now talk of joining with such a one? I am shamed. I have spoken."

"There is only one thing that I know," Two Ponies said with a sigh after Buffalo Udder handed him the pipe. "The Badger Society cannot stand aside and watch. There are three choices before us. We can continue on to the north to join our cousins and fight the Chippewa. We can join Wild Dog, who has no respect for our laws and customs, and try to run the white man from the land. Or we can join the white-eyes and avenge the death of our brothers, as our law demands. I have spoken."

Chapter Eight

The sodbuster stood there next to his crops and shook his head, his arms across his chest.

"I ain't goin' no place," he told Eli Holten. "I've got more work than I know what to do with. I got pigs ta slop and crops to tend to. I can't go galavantin' off 'cause the Army's runnin' scared."

"At least two homesteads have been burned," the scout informed the farmer. "And Wild Dog is headed this way. He attacked us last night."

"The Oglala're my friends," the farmer answered. Decisively he turned and headed back for his barn. Eli sighed, reined his horse around and touched heels, headed for the next homestead up the trail.

The answer to his warnings became monotonously the same. The Oglala were trusted friends. No matter how often he pointed out that Wild Dog and most of his followers were totally renegade, ousted by their parent tribes, the stubborn farmers remained unswayed. Any uprising was the Army's business. It was the Army's job to protect people. Frustrated, Eli started back for the relief column.

Samantha waved from the seat of her wagon with a smile that challenged the beauty of the day, despite the heat. Which reminded Eli of the cooking he was headed for when he got back to the fort. That certainly spoiled his morning.

The scout found Estillman once again lost in the now-soiled letter he'd been reading since the beginning of the patrol.

"You know, Lieutenant," Eli stated. "If reading depressed me that much, I wouldn't read."

"Who asked for your opinion, Scout?" Estillman snapped back. It would have been threatening, but his voice broke on 'Scout.' "What do you have to report?"

"Plenty of farms in the area," Eli answered coolly. "But hardly any of the people plan to join up with us. To a man they say the Indians are their friends."

"With friends like that . . ." Estillman nodded and slipped the letter back into its envelope, putting it in place over his heart.

"My orders don't say anything about forcing these people to come with us. Besides, this close to Rawlins, these are the ones I'm least worried about. We'd best high-tail it back to the fort and be glad for what we got."

Andy Cooper rode out ahead of the small wagon train he guided along the northwest trail for Fort Rawlins and once again studied the smoke signals rising above the northern horizon. They couldn't stop now. They shouldn't be more than a day from the fort. Once there, they'd be safe. Maybe the Army would go back and help them find Amy, the little slow-witted girl who had slipped away from the train three nights ago. He thought about the traders who had happened by the same day.

Johnny and Bobby Baxter had assured them the tribes around these parts had been pacified long ago, couldn't be nicer. They had allayed his fears, even gone out looking for little Amy. But now, the signs said a war party lurked nearby. Up ahead, the wagon master saw a number of Indians suddenly appear, painted for war. More rapidly showed on the horizon, bows and rifles in hand.

He had to get back to the wagons. A circle had to be formed. Cooper turned his horse slowly around, hoping not to arouse the savages. Too late.

The braves began to yip and howl and charge at him. Cooper spurred his animal hard and it leapt toward the wagons. He pulled his revolver as warriors began to flood onto the trail, blocking his route to the train. He fired a shot at them, and it served two purposes. It alerted the men back at the wagons, who, already itchy about the smoke signs and the Indian rider who ran along the southern horizon, immediately started to form a circle. It also got the young wagon master a hail of arrows and bullets that pincushioned him and his horse, thus sparing him from being captured and tortured to a horrible end.

No sooner had the six wagons circled up than a horde of charging warriors descended on them. The occupants of the Conestogas fell out, pulling readied rifles that began to bark at the Indians as they circled the train. Flaming arrows and hot lead began to pour into the horses and covered wagons. The water supply was quickly exhausted on the flames and two of the highsided vehicles burned out of control.

Desperately the setttlers battled. The women reloaded the weapons, the men, many wounded and bleeding, hid under the running gear or behind dead horses still hitched to the rigs, firing into the uncounted numbers of braves.

One shrieking warrior jumped his horse over a prone animal and ran through the inner circle. He buried his lance in a young girl who ran screaming past him. A woman fired a musket she had just reloaded, at point blank range into his side. For a second the painted Oglala froze, the bullet deep in his bowels, then he calmly pulled his rusty revolver and shot the woman in the face. A moment later he slid off his horse and into the spirit world.

A wagoneer stood on the seat of his schooner, firing and reloading his Winchester until the barrel grew too hot to hold. He paused to change weapons and an arrow hit him in the throat. His repeater dropped to the ground. Unnoticed by the harried defenders, he followed shortly after. He wrestled unconsciously in his death throes to dislodge the arrow.

The battle had started late in the day. Dusk quickly approached. The settlers prayed for dark, in the false belief the Indians would not fight at night.

The immigrants' numbers dwindled quickly, however. The Indians knew how many they faced now and, sensing victory, redoubled their attack. One white man, blood streaming from his shoulder, face white, ran from body to body, looking for a rifle that was still loaded. A woman greedily hid a revolver with two rounds left as she hugged her eleven-year-old daughter close. While she watched in horror, the resistance grew sporadic.

More war ponies entered the beleaguered circle. One man jumped from a wagon as a brave rode by and cracked the butt of his rifle across the Indian's face. Three arrows caught the pilgrim in the chest and under his arm almost simultaneously. The warrior he attacked, his skull split, flipped backward over the rump of his pony. In blank-faced stupor, the white people of the train, once the dreamers of farms and ranches and new beginnings, the challengers of a wilderness, waited for the final assault.

It came as dusk took hold. A few scattered shots

from the canvas-topped prairie schooners and then there was no resistance.

Thirty braves rushed in a body around the many dead and the charcoaled wagons, then pranced toward the few Conestogas still intact. The mother calmly thumbed back the hammer on the big Colt she hid.

She placed the muzzle against her trembling daughter's beautifully shaped head and pulled the trigger. Followed by searing hot gasses, the bullet smacked into the eleven-year-old's right ear and blew out the other side, taking the top of the girl's head off. Out burst blood and watery fluid, smoke and gore that splattered along the ground and over her mother's dress. The force of the shot caused the child to bounce away from her mother, then she lay in the dust twitching.

Wild Dog's braves jumped with the unexpected shot. Immediately their rifles came up and they spotted the white woman with the smoking revolver. She smiled defiantly, although her hands shook as she placed the barrel of the recocked weapon in her mouth. She pulled the trigger.

The hammer fell, though the expected shot didn't come. A defective round. She screamed in horror as she tried to cock the hammer again. Then the laughing warriors had her feet and dragged her out from under the wagon. She screamed and threw the useless weapon at the first brave, who boomed with hilarity at the stinging strike, leaned down and punched her hard in the belly.

After that they had little trouble with this one, although the four other women screamed for mercy as their clothes were torn off their backs. Their shrieks of agony increased in volume with each brutal penetration of their dry passages. One-Eye enthusiastically rammed himself into an eighteen-year-old newly-wed, whose firm buttocks slapped against the hard ground as the warrior ground to completion.

Johnny Baxter had been right, he thought with satisfaction. Every one of the white women was a pleasure to be explored. The three surviving men screamed in agony nearby as their wounds were teased. The braves who worked on this laughed with each shout of pain that the whites so liberally gave up. Their torture lasted most of the night. One brave gathered the six children together and found horses to load them on, then rode off with his prize, not waiting for the others. He could get many ponies trading them to people who had lost sons or daughters.

Behind the enterprising fellow, the warriors picked through the unburned wagons, finding bottles of whiskey and finery of all sorts. What were once valuable family heirlooms they absently threw over their shoulders. The braves found gold coin and stripped gold and silver off the bodies as they scalped the dead settlers, remembering Wild Dog exhorting them to bring these things to him.

As the renegades became drunk and occupied themselves with the white women who had finally exhausted their lungs and now only whimpered at the violation they suffered, the depths of a water barrel stirred. From its nearly empty interior rose a small figure who slipped noiselessly from the cask, stole out of the circle of wagons and headed northwest.

The victory celebration lasted until morning, when the last woman bled to death from her uncounted rapes. Once dead, the warrior most deserving scraped the circular cut along the crown of her skull and peeled the roof of the woman's head free of its hair. One man stubbornly lived on, his tongue slashed lengthwise, his lids sliced off and his eyes poked out.

They scalped him as he screamed anew, then they threw him in one of the wagons and set it ablaze.

No whites, Wild Dog had demanded, were to survive.

E Troop led the rag-tag refugees into the compound of the fort half an hour before sundown. The scout had mixed emotions about riding through the gates to the parade ground. Who did he stand a better chance with? Wild Dog on the outside, or Sally Sue, White Doe and Samantha Everett on the inside? Eli noted the parapets had been manned to the teeth. Smoke stained the sky far to the southeast. Wild Dog had covered a lot of ground.

Lieutenant Estillman, Leary and the scout, reported to the general while troopers on disciplinary duty led their horses to the corral, unsaddled them, cleaned and put up the tack. Eli nervously reconnoitered the ground he had to cover to get to the headquarters building, and made a point to stand between the two officers, although Estillman's five foot nine height offered little cover for the six-one frontiersman.

The general stared out the window at the smudge in the distance as the three men presented themselves.

"We had a report that a wagon train was coming in today or tomorrow," Corrington stated with his back to them, while he stayed at the window, not even offering a greeting or returning a salute. "It didn't show. That smoke started half an hour ago."

He turned back to his subordinates and exchanged military courtesies, then pointed to the southeast. "I've sent a patrol to investigate, though I'm assuming that's the wagon train."

He gusted a tired sigh as he took his leather-bound

chair and directed the men to also sit. "How did your mission go?"

Eli started first, reporting the death of Gray Otter and his sons. The general scowled anew.

Estillman gave a quick, terse report. He counted off those settlers whom they had brought in, why some did not come. He related the confrontation E Troop had with the hostiles, named the two dead men, the dead boys and ended with one woman dead, another raped. After a deep breath, he listed the military casualties. Corrington's face blackened.

"You mean you left white people out there?" he fumed.

"General, they wouldn't come," Holten defended. "Short of physical force, some of them would not budge. Like idiots, they insisted that since some Indians are their friends, all Indians would be."

"Estillman, you're going out again bright and early tomorrow," Corrington ordered angrily. "Under the powers of martial law, I'm decreeing that a state of emergency exists. You will bring all the settlers in, with or without their valuables, by force if necessary."

"Yes, sir," Estillman answered red-faced.

"Holten," the general continued. "I want you to get a few good men together and scout out the location of this Wild Dog. Take any man you need on this post."

"Yes, General," Holten answered.

"I've had to order the Hearst wagon train to stay here until this uprising is put down. So I imagine you'll be glad to get out before Sally Sue's family can find you." The general looked Eli straight in the eyes and the scout could clearly read the cold thoughts that haunted his mind.

"Find this monster, Eli," the general urged. "This is turning into a blood-bath."

Chapter Nine

The scout asked for two men, Sergeant Patrick Andrews and Corporal Warren Murphy.

"You don't believe in leaving me much, do you, Scout?" Estillman noted wryly as he, Eli and Lieutenant Leary headed out the door of the general's office.

"I know Morrison is not available, or I'd have chosen him first. For something like this only the best will do." Eli stated thoughtfully, then shrugged. "Those two will have to do."

One other piece of business had to be taken care of, and Eli did not look forward to it.

With the cover of darkness, the scout slipped to his cabin. He didn't enter. Instead he found a vantage point from which he could observe the entrance. Exactly on the hour, five hulking forms loomed out of the shadows and marched to the front of his quarters.

Matthew stepped forward and threw the door open. A tirade of angry Lakota rattled out at the family, along with a stream of household objects. Matthew reshut the door.

"Not here, Paw," the son reported.

"Let's go around the officers quarters," Adam Hearst suggested. "Then the stables. He may be sleeping with his horse."

"Why not?" Mark shot back. "He sleeps with everything else."

The Hearst clan trudged off.

Eli slipped to the door, pressed the wooden latch and slid inside—to be clobbered with a tin pan.

White Doe put her hands to her mouth, eyes wide with surprise.

"Tall Bear!" she exclaimed.

"Ow!" Eli responded, rubbing the shoulder where the tin wash basin had struck.

"I thought the wed-din' men had come again," she explained by way of apology. Her eyes filled with concern as she drew close. "I have hurt you."

"No," Eli assured her, "but I have very bad news."

They sat on the edge of the bed, while Eli told her of what he knew of her father and brothers. White Doe took the news stoically.

"I knew they would not join Wild Dog after what he did to a great chief." White Doe sighed and rested her head on Eli's chest, moisture soaked into his flannel shirt.

"I have to pick up some supplies," Eli said softly, holding the Indian girl close, "then I have to go."

"No!" White Doe jumped back, determination in her eyes. "You must stay! I have missed you. I have lain here on this sagging-place-to-sleep and dreamt of you being there instead of my fingers." Her brown eyes became deep pools of desperation.

"Can you not stay with me for at least a little while?" she pleaded.

Eli's whipcord trousers grew tight as his fleshy lance became stiff. He looked down at his traitorous crotch with disgust.

"You get me in more trouble," he growled, then decided as he watched White Doe begin to undress that it was the kind of trouble he went looking for.

Quickly he pulled his heavy turnip watch out and took note of the time.

"We have fifty-two minutes," he told White Doe. Though the words meant nothing to her, a smile blossomed on her face and she began pulling at Eli's clothes.

The energetic girl was like a wagon wheel freshly greased, her silky gate to paradise lubricated with passion. Pleasantries were abandoned, although White Doe didn't seem to notice. She squealed with delight as Eli coupled with her. Strong, muscular legs wrapped around his back. A sudden gasp and shudder from White Doe let Eli know the beautiful Oglala had missed him greatly and her expectations had at least been partially fulfilled.

Then the door burst open.

Eli looked to see Sally Sue inside the entranceway, her legs spread slightly, her jaw slack above her ample chest and her eyes bulging out of her head. Her surprised squeak turned to a groan and she began to step back out of the cabin.

"Sally Sue, wait!" Eli turned to extract himself from White Doe but she was drunk on her passion and had not even heard the white girl enter the cabin. She held on tightly with legs and arms. Eli struggled to his knees and found a cheek of White Doe's rump in each of his hands as the girl sat on his shaft, grunting with pleasure at the new position.

Suddenly he had a wild urge to scream, "Sally Sue, I can explain."

Civilization, he thought bitterly. The Hearsts, and people like them, had brought *civilization* to the plains and, with it, all the hypocrisy that any place needed. White Doe, only a year older than Sally Sue, found no one putting pressure on Holten to marry her. Such an idea was not civilized. Even he, Holten

ealized, found himself slipping into the charades of
polite society.

"If you tell your brothers," Eli warned around
White Doe's bobbing head, "they're gonna kill me."

The white girl froze a moment, then her face
twisted with jealousy. "What she got that I don't?" she
wailed.

"It's not what she's got, it's what she don't have
. ." Eli countered. "Lots of brothers and marriage
ambitions."

Sally Sue's face hardened and she closed the door
behind her. "You're mine," she charged as she began
tugging at the buttons on her dress. "She can't have
you."

White Doe squealed anew with the lengthening rod
as Eli watched Sally Sue shake her bloomers from her
hips. The gauntlet had been thrown, the challenge
issued. The scout found himself anticipating the joust.

White Doe turned her head and out of lust-glazed
eyes studied her competitor. Not so bad, she thought.
But so pale, like dough-cakes. Sally Sue circled warily,
looking for an opening. She slid lazily, disarmingly up
against Eli's back.

"Finish up on her," the blonde wanton cooed into
Eli's ear. "Then it's my turn."

Time got muddled in the free-for-all that followed.
The contest between the girls turned into a giggling
match, each vying for Eli's attention, each girl
working to keep his fiery hunger burning and his
tempting snake rigid with excitement. Only when the
shuddering and gasps of blissful completion came did
one or the other of them relinquish the match.

Eli, though, couldn't lose as his own crest
approached for the third time. Flat on his back,
White Doe again on his bolt of ecstasy, Sally Sue
moaning over him as he played his tongue along the

petals of her silken tunnel. He approached the pinnacle of the mountain and discovered it to be a volcano that erupted in flaming liquids. White Doe: Three; Sally Sue: Nothing. But not from lack of trying.

A polite knock sounded at the door, but no one inside heard.

Samantha Everett stepped through the portal of the cabin. She struck the same pose as Sally Sue when the girl made her great discovery.

Eli could see Samantha around Sally Sue's thighs and groaned. Lord, please, he thought prayerfully, not another one.

His petition could have been answered in a better manner. Matthew Hearst pushed past the widow Everett.

The world went black as Sally Sue sat down on his head.

"Quick!" he heard her muffled voice cry out. "I got 'im pinned. Whatever you do, don't hurt him."

Samantha watched the bruiser at the door turn back outside and say with an even, absent voice, "He's here, Pa."

Sally Sue went flying off the bed, White Doe fell to a corner as Eli wrestled to his own defense, stripped of all his weapons. Matthew and Mark were already inside, Luke stood in the opening. With a leap, Eli got to the door and snapped a foot to the inside of Luke's thigh. The boy doubled up and Eli slammed the door against his head, bolting him out with John and Adam Hearst.

Mark brought up his shotgun. The scout slipped past and grabbed the long barrel of the Parker while he slammed his whole body against the Hearst boy. Mark wheezed and gasped for air as Eli swung the shotgun like a club.

The wood stock caught Matthew in the head. The eldest Hearst boy bounced off a wall and staggered, dazed, toward the door. He lost a tooth when someone on the outside tried to smash it open. Eli turned and delivered a wound-up fist to Mark's head. All the while he kept reminding himself that he really didn't want to hurt them, only keep *them* from hurting *him*.

The boy stumbled back, slapped his head hard against the wall and struggled to keep his feet. White Doe solved that problem by winding up a cast iron skillet in a two-hand hold and landing the edge of it in Mark's breadbasket. He doubled over with a whoosh and the Indian girl cracked the frying pan as hard as she could against the back of his head. Mark Hearst slumped to the floor and didn't move.

"Eli!" Samantha screamed. She pointed at the door where a shotgun barrel probed past.

Holten grabbed the double barrels and jerked the weapon forward. It brought Luke with it. Eli slammed the door behind Luke and heard someone get smacked. A yelp of pain preceded the sound of staggering footsteps.

"Don't fire that gun in there, boy," Adam's voice boomed through the door. "Think of your sister."

"Yes, sir," Luke answered an instant before Eli swung Luke's Parker overhead. He cracked the Hearst boy on the hard top of his head and drove him to his knees. Holten brought the shotgun around again and finished the job with a lateral butt stroke to the jaw. Luke fell unceremoniously on his face.

Eli searched around him. There was no fight left in the Hearst boys. The scout patted himself on the back. Not one of them had laid a fist on him. Before he could move, though, Adam Hearst slammed into the door. It swatted against Eli's back and threw him to the bed.

111

Father Hearst stepped through the entrance, his son John lying prone outside, one too many doors slammed against his face. "You're marryin' my daughter," Adam growled as he raised his shotgun and began to ear the hammers back.

Samantha, who had been in a corner behind the door, threw her weight against it now. She couldn't hope to move the antagonist with her slight weight, but she did distract him for a moment.

Eli surged from his prone position and, in one lunge, slapped the Hearst's patriarch alongside the head.

Adam Hearst came of sterner stuff than his sons. He rolled his eyes, spat blood on the floor and dropped his engraved Parker. With what appeared to be a casual swing, he belted Holten across the room, where the scout landed next to the naked Sally Sue.

"Eli," she said with a smile. "I'd like you to meet my Papa."

"We've met," Eli wheezed.

"But not formally introduced," she explained.

Holten struggled to his feet. For the first time he realized that he, too, was naked. Undaunted, he launched himself again at the father of the would-be bride.

"Get him, Eli!" White Doe shouted in Lakota. "Beat the weddin' man."

Eli landed a solid blow against Adam's gut. It felt like punching a tree. Hearst grunted and threw a straight punch at Holten's head. The scout slipped the blow. It bounced off his shoulder as Eli tried again to make an impression on Adam's stomach. Failing this, he leaned back and delivered a solid upper-cut to the chin.

Adam stumbled back toward the door. The scout moved with him and delivered a fusillade of quick, tight one-two punches to the older man's ribs, then grabbed Adam by his shirt and cracked a solid blow to his face.

A puzzled expression crossed Adam Hearst's face, as if he didn't actually believe this had happened. Then his eyes rolled up and he sank to his knees. A slight nudge from Holten and he crashed onto his side.

"I'm never gonna get married," Sally Sue wailed.

"Yes, you will, Sally Sue," Eli comforted as he pulled on his trousers. "Just not to me."

"Good," White Doe chortled suddenly, not understanding a word of English, save one. "You beat the wed-ding people."

Samantha stepped out of the corner of the room, arms crossed. The fire in her eyes burned holes in the scout's chest. He tried to ignore her while he worked stockinged feet into his boots. A still-naked White Doe gathered up the rest of his clothes and placed them on the bed. Eli nervously pulled his shirt on as the widow woman stood before him.

"Maybe I should have mentioned my problems back here at the fort," Holten finally volunteered as he slipped his belt on.

"Oh, Eli," Samantha burbled. "I never thought I owned you. I never dreamed I was the only one."

The scout felt a warm glow. Someone had finally offered him a kind, understanding word.

"But . . . two at a time!" the widow shrieked. "And they're mere babies, both of them. Eli Holten, you're sick."

The widow Everett stomped out of the cabin. The door slammed violently after her and one leather hinge sagged threateningly. First Sergeant Morrison stalked to the door, a length of two-by-four in his beefy fist. He surveyed the prone Hearsts, tipped his hat to the still-naked Sally Sue and walked over to where Eli sat.

"And ta think I was worried about ya," the Irishman chuckled.

The five man patrol rode hard toward the front gate of Fort Rawlins, a small boy in the lap of Corporal Beulow. He shouted to the guard above the entrance and one giant door swung partially open. The troopers gigged their animals through. Eli and E Troop's first sergeant came running toward the commotion.

The dull-hurt eyes of the six-year-old boy looked blankly around. His face crumpled and tears threatened.

"Found him two hours out of here, runnin' up the trail," the corporal offered. "We heard Indians up ahead, so I turned back."

"Why wasn't a whole troop sent?" a civilian shouted from the gathering crowd.

"Because there's close to a hundred hostiles out there and I'm not about to commit an entire troop to the dark," General Corrington growled as he pushed through the onlookers. They grumbled some, though quietly.

Eli took the boy into his arms and carried him over to the dispensary. The regimental doctor already had been awakened and waited at the medical facility.

"A few cuts, some bruises from falling as he ran along the trail," the surgeon declared. "Nothing serious."

General Corrington entered the room and bent down to eye level with the child to study the still-dulled eyes. "What's your name, boy?"

"Tommy," he answered flatly.

"What happened?" the general pressed. The boy's

114

eyes grew big.

"Momma screamed forever," he whispered.

The general backed away, averting his eyes. Eli took his place.

"Did the Indians come?" he asked. The boy nodded.

"Daddy put me in a water barrel," Tommy volunteered. "He told me to stay there until all the noise stopped, then head the way we'd been goin'."

"Are you hungry?" Eli asked after a pause. Tommy nodded again.

"Then I'm going to get First Sergeant Morrison to take you over to the mess hall and get you something to eat."

"They took all my friends away," Tommy offered.

"Who?"

"All the other kids. They loaded 'em on horses and took 'em all away."

"How many?" the general asked.

The boy raised five fingers on one hand and a spare one on the other. Frank Corrington shook his head in defeat. He felt his whole department was falling apart around him.

Sergeant Morrison took the lad into his arms. "C'mon, me bucko," he crooned. "Let the ol' sergeant git ye somethin' ta eat."

"My Dearest Loren," the new letter started, and the rest read as a not-so-veiled ultimatum. A young lawyer, someone Estillman knew from his secondary school days, had been taking Deborah to the functions she was obliged to attend. She found, or so she claimed, his goals in life more in tune with her own. It only emphasized, to her, the vast difference with Loren's. She still loved her dreamer of a betrothed,

115

she wanted him to understand, her fine officer in the handsome dress uniform. But . . ." Eli's knock ended his doleful reading.

The scout leaned into the room. "The general wants to see us, Estillman. It's an emergency."

"Thank you, Chief Scout," Loren answered as he refolded the letter and put it over his heart. "If you'll wait a moment, I'll walk with you."

"You know, Lieutenant," Eli dared to venture. "That letter isn't going to change its words."

"You'll be glad to know, Mr. Holten," Estillman said evenly, "that I have a new letter to grieve over in the field."

The general's mood could not have been blacker. "I should have sent a troop," he mourned, his eyes studying the floor.

"It was already too late, Frank," Holten suggested. "They would've been targets out there in the dark."

"I'm sending A Troop out tomorrow at the crack of dawn," Corrington ordered. "It will investigate this wagon train and try to pursue the hostiles, round up any settlers in the area . . . and look for the children." He sighed and began to pour brandy, a sure sign that the hard job would come their way.

"I want everyone to look for the children. Eli, I want you to take more men with you. Two isn't enough if you locate the hostiles . . . or the children. I want you to go ahead of E Troop and look around. Estillman, I want you to *hurry* and get those settlers in. From now on, we are quick and we are ruthless."

Boots and Saddles played an hour before the sun shone. Troops A and E lined up for inspection. Estillman sat quietly on his horse, the excitement he'd felt the last time gone with his worries. The sergeants did

116

their usual growling to get the men ready to move out.

Warren Murphy approached the scout with three more men, Sergeant Andrews from E Troop, the other two from other units. "They're the best ah know, Mr. Holten," the ex-rebel bragged. "And Ah'd be willin' ta throw my life in with them."

"You probably will," Eli countered as he gained his saddle.

Murphy brought his horse around to the scout's left side and a clinking sounded when the two mounts brushed. Eli, curious, tapped the bulging saddle bags on the brown gelding the corporal sported. The ring of glass rose through the leather.

"Corporal, you seem to be carrying a great deal of breakables," Eli observed. The ex-Confederate nervously thinned his lips.

"Mr. Holten, sir," he answered. "Ah'm carryin' everythin' necessary for sustainin' the life in an Ahrishman. Sergeant Morrison hates to admit it, but Ah shoa am Ahrish." His blue eyes twinkled and his lined cheeks writhed with merriment.

Eli studied the soldier's face.

"Well, it's gonna be a long campaign," Murphy continued. "Ah can tell these things."

Holten thought about it for a moment, shrugged and reined his horse to the right. "I just hope it's *good* Irish whiskey."

"That it is, suh, that is it," Murphy responded with a smile of relief.

With the false dawn, A Troop paraded past the headquarters' building, two abreast, and out the gate to the accompaniment of the regimental music and color guard. Also a few sarcastic remarks from early-rising civilians. They headed northeast. Estillman's troops marched due west, Eli and his five picked men ranged out ahead.

117

"Do you know what's eating the lieutenant, Corporal?" Eli asked Warren Murphy as they cantered along.

"It must be woman trouble, although from lookin' at him, ya wouldn't think he'd know what to do with one," Murphy answered. "Yuh know, Ah smell a good man somewhere in thet boy's face, the way he handles hisself an' all, but theh's a piece missin' from the Loren Estillman puzzle an' Ah'll be damned tuh know what thet piece is."

Eli and his hand-picked men pushed so far ahead of the Troop that they were nearly to the Cheyenne River fork when they made camp for the night. Estillman intended to repeat his previous tactic and herd the homesteaders in from the outermost fringe first. Eli settled down to try to make a decent meal out of what he had in his supplies. In the summer, the smaller animals of the plains were infested with worms and diseases that made them inedible and no one had thought to stop by some farm to purchase fresh meat.

"Well, now, Chief Scout, Mr. Holten," Warren Murphy proclaimed as he sat down next to Eli at the fire. "I have somethin' most refreshin' here that assists in makin' the awful more bearable."

The flask came out of the good corporal's hip pocket and Eli smiled appreciatively.

"It's bound to help," Sergeant Andrews said, joining the two at the fire, his hand out for the container of whiskey.

"Don't be gettin' grabby, Sergeant," Murphy snapped.

"You wouldn't deny a man refreshment, would you, Murphy? Particularly if he outranks you?" Andrews returned sweetly, his sandy hair and pale blue eyes marking his ancestry.

"No. I wouldn't begrudge my comrades in arms a

118

drink. Even a hard-headed Scotsman like yerself."

"Well said, for an Orangeman with, like as not, Scots blood in him," Andrews gave him back.

"Hold it." Eli tapped a finger to his lips, then pointed past the clearing that still enjoyed a small amount of the light of day. Murphy immediately understood and snapped open the holster flap over his Colt revolver. Andrews did the same as he rose and moved back evenly to where the three other men stood bedding down the horses. Eli motioned the Irish Confederate to move to the right, while he came silently to his feet and started to the left.

The faint noise he had heard came again, this time loud enough for everyone to take note.

Eli slid into the light brush at the edge of the small clearing they had chosen and squinted into the failing light in an effort to see detail in the denser parts of the growth.

More motion. Away from him now, closer to camp. He listened for other intruders around the clearing. Only one, he decided with relief a moment later, and this was one making enough noise to silence the chirping of the crickets.

Suddenly, from the other side of the bushes, came a whoop, a youthful shout of surprise and anger and a wild Rebel yell that startled the birds out of the trees.

"Ah got 'im. Ah got the little devil!" Murphy bellowed as he carried a squirming Indian boy into the camp. "Ah don' believe it. They've sent a chile to scalp me."

The crushing beefy arms of the corporal pinned the struggling boy, slender and wiry, no more than twelve, against the Orangeman's chest. The youngster's arms flailed ineffectually at the air.

"Let him go, Murphy," Eli said, signing a greeting to the youth.

"But the squirmy monster'll get away," Murphy protested.

"Not until he delivers his message," Eli answered. "He's not a full-fledged warrior, or else we'd've never heard him." The corporal put the boy down. In Lakota, Holten greeted the messenger once more.

"I am Tall Bear," the scout started. "I would welcome you to our camp, but you tried to sneak up and attack us."

"I did not intend to attack," the boy protested in a high voice, then his cheeks grew darker. "I am Walking Hawk. I practiced my silent steps just now in the brush."

"You *need* the practice," the scout chided gently. "What brings you here then, if not for our scalps?"

"I carry a message from Two Ponies, Chief of the Badger Society. He wishes to speak with Tall Bear, friend of the Oglala."

"Do you know what he desires to speak to me about?" Eli inquired. The young boy nodded.

"It is about Wild Dog and how to stop this bad medicine."

"Fellas," Holten turned to his men with a smile. "We're goin' to a pow-wow."

Chapter Ten

Two Ponies had scheduled the meeting for a spot a mile north from the ruins of the first homestead Wild Dog had wiped out. Eli knew, for courtesy's sake, he was expected to bring a feast. Early the next morning the five out-riders galloped back to the troop as it prepared to turn around and head back, collecting the remaining settlers—by force if necessary—and removing them from the hostile area. Eli reported to Estillman and told him about the meeting.

"Do you wish me to go along?" the youthful lieutenant asked.

"Best thing, in my opinion, is for me to take my four men and you keep on rounding up the settlers," Eli answered. "It may still be a trap. In any event, I'm going to be expected to bring some food."

"What sort of food?" Estillman inquired.

"A feast. Plenty meat . . . coffee . . . lots of sugar," Eli qualified.

"We've got ample of the last two. As to the meat . . . good luck."

Two hours later, E Troop rode into Orsen Brunnen's pig farm looking for more than just to round the man up. As it turned out, the Brunnen family was ready to move.

"I hear about the immigrant train," the German

explained as he threw his belongings into the back of a wagon. A large blonde-haired woman with over-ample breasts marched out of the soddy, hauling a gigantic smoked ham. Brunnen nodded to her.

"Diss ist mine wife, Ilsa," he introduced over his shoulder. The woman frowned and glared at Estillman and Holten. They tipped their hats to her. Another woman came out of the pig corrals. A girl really, of about eighteen, a good five foot eleven inches, with Nordic features, blonde hair braided into pig-tails on both sides of her head, wearing overalls.

"Und dis ist mine daughter, Helga," Brunnen announced. "Helga, *disen Herren sind Herr Holten und Leutenent Estillman. Sie, wirt Uns nach der festunges aufnehmen.*"

Helga had a weaner pig tucked under one arm, its front legs clamped tightly together by her hand. Her full, pink cheeks and high forehead were smudged with dirt. Estillman smiled politely and tipped his cap.

"How do you do, Miss Brunnen," he said absently.

Helga didn't answer for a moment. Her sparkling eyes had locked on the small lieutenant and her deep blue gaze glazed over as she studied him.

"*G-Gutt, danke* . . . er, g-good, thank you. H-how do you do, Lieutenant?" she stammered out.

"Very pleased to meet you," Estillman continued cordially.

"We also need to make a purchase, Mr. Brunnen," Eli continued. "We're going to be meeting with some potential Indian allies and I need to bring something to eat."

"Eat? Buy? Of course. I have some smoked ham, some bacon maybe?"

Helga had as yet to move. She stood like a cow at the slaughterhouse, staring. Estillman was dead in her sights.

"Live pigs," Eli qualified. "I know they'd prefer buffalo, but we'll have to make do with fresh pork."

"Oot uf de question," Brunnen exploded. "All uf mine pigs ist too young. I drive dem to der fort. Den, if I vait anodder eight, ten months, mine profits vill be much larger."

"But, sir," Estillman appealed. "We need those pigs now."

Eli did a double-take as he noticed the mooning Helga. He followed the gaze to Estillman and smiled knowingly.

"Nein! Nein!" Orsen Brunnen shouted adamantly. "Ve vill sell no swine before its time."

"But, Mr. Brunnen," Estillman protested. Eli interrupted him.

"Never mind, Lieutenant. We'll just have to pick up something else."

"Only that'll take . . ." Eli silenced the lieutenant with a lifted hand and turned away from the farmer. Puzzled, Estillman followed. They trotted to First Sergeant Morrison's side.

"Sergeant," Eli confided. "Mr. Brunnen is a bit reluctant to sell us any of his pigs, so we're going to have to find something else."

"What? Ah, it's a shame it tiz," Morrison exclaimed bitterly. "An' here I was all ready for some roasted pork."

"So, let me put this in your hands," Holten continued. "Find us something else, perhaps . . . the same as . . . two, no make it three pigs, fairly big."

"Now, where would I be findin' anythin' like that in this God-forsaken . . ." Michael Delehanty Morrison, pride of Killarney, stopped in mid-sentence, a glint gaining a place in his eyes. He smiled broadly.

"Ah, you can leave it to me, Mr. Holten. You might not suspect such a thin', but I got a little bit a' Irish gypsy in me blood."

"You might ask Miss Helga Brunnen, the handsome, *large* lady over there, if she might be able to help you." Eli leaned closer from the back of his horse toward the Irishman-turned-Gypsy. "Tell her that her help would be seen as a special favor to Lieutenant Loren Estillman."

The young officer inclined forward, into the conversation.

"What?" he asked eloquently.

Eli winked at the sergeant, who glanced toward the still-mooning Helga and the lieutenant.

"Oh, Lieutenant, darlin'," Morrison chortled. "You dee'vil you."

"What's he talking about, Chief Scout?" the confused young man inquired.

Eli and the lieutenant waited patiently to the east of the Brunnen farm in a slight wash. The scout held the reins of Morrison's horse, which munched absently on grass, while Estillman made terrible company, lost in a moment of black self-pity. At last he came out of it, to complain once again.

"I still don't know what this is about. Or why I have to be here."

Thrashing, grunting animals nearby announced the arrival of Sergeant Morrison.

The Irishman pushed through to the wash with a struggling weaner in his arms. Behind him came Helga Brunnen with two more pigs on ropes. The sergeant wore a satisfied expression and Helga wore radiance like the blush of spring.

She had washed and stuffed her ample frame into a lovely white cotton dress with simple blue flowers sprinkling the hems and collar. It had to be her best dress. She'd come barefoot, hoping to downplay her unfeminine height. Matching blue ribbons sparkled in her hair, that she had coiled in a large, single braid around her head like a golden crown.

"There we be, Lieutenant," Morrison growled in his version of a whisper. "And all because o' this fine lady." The sergeant bowed to the German girl, who nervously bit her lip and stared boldly up at Estillman.

Loren, barely stirred from his somber thoughts, struggled to tip his cap politely to the lady and mumbled, "Thank you."

"Oh, but it vas mine pleasure," Helga breathed expectantly. She stepped up next to Estillman's horse. "Mine vater does not understand, und besides, I vould do anythink for der . . . *the* Army." She smiled with puppydog eyes. "I lof' to see a man in uniform."

Morrison grinned impishly behind her and swelled his chest as he slipped the stolen pig under one arm and began to brush the front of his uniform. He nodded sagely to Holten.

"Especially an officer's uniform," Helga amended.

Morrison missed a beat in his brushing, winked at the scout and switched the snorting animal to the other arm.

"Naturally, we'll pay a fair price for the swine," Estillman said flatly. He reached into his pocket for an Army requisition form and a stub of pencil. Swiftly he wrote out the date, place and amount, tore it off and handed it to the girl. Helga glanced nervously toward the soddy.

"I should be getting back," she announced, smiled sweetly and looked hopefully at the young officer.

"*Aber,* a young lady should not be valking alone in such times," she went on. Then she held her breath. Estillman's dark thoughts had not cleared his mind, though, and his answer crushed all her hopes.

"You're quite right, Miss Brunnen. I'm sure the sergeant will escort you home safely."

The hurt expression in Helga's eyes seemed nothing compared to Morrison's mixture of incredulous disbelief and surprise. Helga dropped her head and eyed the ground, her pink cheeks blushing red. The first sergeant recovered from his dismay.

"Well, Lieutenant Estillman, sir," the Irish non-com stated with calculating fire in his eyes as he offered a hand to Helga. "It will be an honor, sir, an' a privilege to walk such a handsome young lady as Miss Brunnen anywhere she'd like ta go, sir."

Eli took the three pigs, having to slip an extra rope around the sergeant's ward, then Morrison and the dejected Helga began to walk back to the Brunnen soddy.

"That was rather rude, Lieutenant," Eli said icily, once the pair had gone out of sight and hearing.

"Humm?" Estillman responded, only then coming completely out of his dismal thoughts and startled to see three squirming pigs in the scout's care.

"You know damned well what I'm talking about," Eli continued, irritation surfacing in his words. "That young lady wanted *you* to walk her home. She's, ah, smitten, sir."

Loren Estillman gritted his teeth and his eyes flamed. "You mean me on the ground, shaded by her breasts, Mr. Holten? While she towers over me and I have to take three steps to her one? You mean that kind of a walk?" he complained, then leaned toward the scout and stabbed a finger at his chest.

"Don't you think I'm aware—painfully aware—of my height? And this damned voice. I'm lucky to have one woman who . . ." he broke off suddenly, achingly aware of the uncertainty of that prospect. "Go feed

126

your Indian friends, Scout!"

Estillman whirled his horse and cantered toward the relief force. Holten stood in his stirrups.

"Shit!" he exploded, then shouted after the lieutenant. "Real men don't worry about things like that!"

Holten waited for the first sergeant to return. Between them they carried the three pigs to where Corporal Murphy and the four chosen soldiers waited. Morrison wished them luck and the six rode to a mile of where Eli had been told they would find Two Ponies' camp.

"I want you to wait here with the men, Sergeant," Eli told Andrews. "If I don't come back, you'll know it was a trap. You should get back to Estillman and tell him that he's on his own."

Murphy looked crestfallen. "We're not goin' with you?" the big corporal exclaimed. "Here I had mah heart set on roast pig, my stomach growls at the thought."

Eli placed a trussed up swine in front and in back of him on his horse. "I knew you would, Corporal," Eli answered with a wink. "That's why I had Morrison get three."

Warren Murphy studied the extra pig and his face beamed with pleasure. "Sure now, an' you're a good man, Scout. If we could fig'er out what's wrong with the little tin god we got fer a commander, E Troop'd be a nice place to live," Murphy said in a fair imitation of the first sergeant.

Chapter Eleven

Holten headed his horse toward Two Ponies' camp and arrived with the bellowing announcement of the *eyanpaha*, the camp crier.

A tall red rock, chiseled into the form of a man, stood at the entrance of a large lodge, his solid features frozen with ritual disdain. Eli knew this man in the stove-pipe hat with the George Washington amulet around his neck to be Two Ponies, the great war leader of the *Ihoka*, the Badger Lodge. With a face he froze to match the leader of the warrior society, Eli dismounted, left the pigs squealing behind and stepped in front of the rock. In the haughty voice of an Oglala fighting man, he announced himself.

"I am Tall Bear, son of Two Horns," he started, his legs spread wide, head cocked defiantly. Then he went on to the war leader, "I have come at the beckoning of the great Two Ponies and I bring a feast."

Two Ponies crossed his arms, a vaguely threatening gesture to make, and answered.

"I am Two Ponies, war chief of the *Ihoka*. We have never met, Tall Bear, but I have heard tell you are an honorable, honest man who speaks from the heart. A rare thing among white men."

"Too rare," Eli answered honestly. "Think of me

also as Oglala."

The chief nodded and the rock face softened as Two Ponies gave a hint of a smile. He grunted pleasure at this meeting, then looked past Eli at the doomed swine.

"Let my women take the feast and prepare it for us while we smoke."

"There is coffee and sugar," Holten informed Two Ponies. "And the sweet, white root that grows in the white man's fields."

"All this is good," Two Ponies agreed. The pigs and saddle bags were hauled off Eli's Morgan. The scout retrieved his Oglala bowl and horn spoon from one leather pouch and followed Two Ponies to his own tipi. The war leader held the flap to the lodge open for Eli to enter, then the two men circled to the right, and Two Ponies directed Eli to the honored guest's spot, to the right of the leader's seat. The powerful young man produced a pipe and a pouch of *knicaknic*. He lighted the longstemmed device and made the ritual puffs to the six directions, drew deeply on the tobacco and willow-bark mixture and passed the feather-decorated pipe to Holten. The scout repeated the ceremony, then the two men sat and smoked quietly. After a long silence, Two Ponies spoke his mind.

"After we eat, I will call my warriors to the council fire and I will ask you to help us decide what to do about Wild Dog."

The bluntness of the statement surprised Eli, though he revealed nothing and Two Ponies did not continue. Instead, they sat in hushed contemplation until the rich scent of roasting pork informed them that the meal would soon be served. Then they spoke of everyday things; the hunting, movement of the buffalo, chances for an early winter. Half a dozen senior members of the society had been invited to the feast and their arrival brought the pipe out again. Two Ponies' wives and daughters served the meal. The eight men ate until they were full, talking of old times and making jokes at each other's expense. Then Two Ponies had the *eyanpaha* call the warriors to the council lodge.

Once again the pipe was passed and it took a long time for all to observe the ritual. When finally the last warrior had smoked, while the keeper of the medicine bundle sang the society's song, Two Ponies, rose, grasping the pipe, and spoke at length.

"I have called Tall Bear here because he is the only one that I have heard of that is both close to the white man soldiers and to the people of the Dakota," the leader began. "I am torn. I am shamed and angered by Wild Dog's actions. He broke the law. The murder of Black Spotted Horse brought dishonor to Wild Dog. He also is responsible for killing Gray Otter and his sons. This, too, robs him of honor. Dishonor has also come to all those Oglala who have done nothing about these crimes. Some tell me that since Wild Dog was once an Oglala, he is still one of us. So I would be guilty of murdering one of my own if I make war on him. Yet, the same persons tell me that since he is no longer one of my tribe, I should not be overly offended because he raided one of our bands. I am told his medicine is powerful and that I should join him because of this. I have received much counselling on this matter." Two Ponies paused and turned to his guest. In a quiet voice he asked him: "Tall Bear, tell me what you think, not just what the white man thinks, but . . . what Tall Bear feels."

Eli suddenly realized he'd been called not only to talk about Wild Dog and what to do about him, but to advise these fierce men of the Badger totem. Two

130

Ponies knew what he wanted to do. The problem lay in convincing the other warriors in the lodge to come with their leader against Wild Dog. The question of joining him did not weigh so heavily as the prospect of simply doing nothing and then to see the young men slipping away one or two at a time to follow the crazed mystic. Holten thought a few hard moments before he picked up the pipe and rose to speak.

"I want the Badger men to know I understand the torn loyalties that you feel." Eli cleared his throat and paused before continuing. "I lived for six years with the Oglala. I know the meaning of family, clan and tribe. Wild Dog's medicine is powerful, that is true. One of the reasons I know this is because he has filled the Oglala with these sundered feelings. I say this is one good reason to make war on Wild Dog. Perhaps the best. Clear your mind of these many opinions and see past them to what makes you think them.

"Wild Dog is a great evil. He tears at the very things that bind you and those good thoughts of honor that at this time make you filled with indecision. His song empties his followers of these noble thoughts. It makes them see only him. Surely a warrior who does not decide what he must do for himself is no longer a man, but a slave. He has lost the essence of an Oglala warrior. He has become another man's dog."

"Many young braves follow Wild Dog," Two Ponies countered after he stood and signed for the pipe in order to speak. "Perhaps it is as you say, that Wild Dog's medicine is bad and he must die. How, in my heart though, do I kill his followers, so many good braves, in order to stop Wild Dog, without betraying the nation?" He handed the pipe back to the scout.

Holten drew a patient breath, knowing that Two Ponies counted on him to answer this question in a way that would silence the opponents in the lodge.

"These young men are misled," Eli said flatly. "The problem can be solved by ridding the plains of Wild Dog. In this way the young warriors will be freed of the bad medicine that Wild Dog sings and they will see reason."

Two Ponies grunted and nodded in agreement.

"We all agree that Wild Dog is evil and deserves to die. Then, let us join together to bring an end to his wrong ways."

"Tall Bear's words are wise. Does Tall Bear mean that he will seek to find Wild Dog and kill him, while sparing the others?"

Two Ponies' words came as a shock. The scout hadn't thought about it like that before. Quickly his mind raced to see the possibilities. He knew it would take some thinking to devise a way.

"It is a good idea," Eli answered tentatively. "I must remind Two Ponies, though, that with each attack on settlers or the Army, the young men with Wild Dog break the treaty they are supposed to abide by and also they break the white man's law. Some sort of punishment will have to fall on them."

A murmur of displeasure ran through the gathered warriors, who had up to now been silent. Eli feared he had said the one thing that would split the lodge worse than it already was, but he couldn't lie to them. He had to tell them all the consequences of Wild Dog's and his followers' actions.

Two Ponies sat quietly, considering this before he rose to speak again.

"It seems right that they be punished for the bad things they do. Still, as you can tell, my brothers do not care for this news."

"I could not lie to them," Eli answered forcefully.

Two Ponies paused again, staring into the fire. Finally he spoke.

"I am committed," he said simply. "I have started this talk and I will continue it . . ."

"No!" a young warrior shouted. He struggled to his feet. "I am Beaver Swimming and I cannot sit silent anymore. Like Small Eagle, I have heard the song of Wild Dog. I do not wish to join him. I do not desire to sing his song. But neither do I wish to kill my brothers who have joined him. If we cannot stay out of this, I must leave my lodge and my band and join the Asiniboine and fight the white man in their way. I have spoken."

Beaver Swimming whirled and charged out the exit, followed by four other young braves, one of them Small Eagle, a smug smirk on his face.

A rumble of displeasure ran through the lodge. The red crag Two Ponies had for a face twisted in anger. "It is this very thing that I have sought to avoid," he said sadly. "What must be, will be and if I and those who follow me are destined to fight our own lodge brothers to stop Wild Dog, we will."

Two Ponies began to pace the lodge, stopped, then turned back to Eli.

"You say the young Oglala men that have joined Wild Dog must be punished, yet nowhere have you said if white men must be punished for joining Wild Dog."

The scout's face registered his surprise.

"White men have joined Wild Dog?" he asked. Two Ponies nodded coldly.

"Two brothers, white men, who are called John-ay and Bob-bee, are selling Wild Dog guns and whiskey. They also bring the medicine man a magic potion that Wild Dog is known to take before he has his visions. It is also said that these men told Wild Dog and One-Eye where to find the rolling wood lodges that they attacked so close to the place the pony soldiers stay.

These white men told Wild Dog how many men and women, guns, horses."

Eli set his gaze on the cold stones Two Ponies had for eyes. "If what you say is true, these two white men will pay more dearly than any Oglala brave. Their necks will be stretched by the rope. This I promise you."

Two Ponies grunted with satisfaction and a ripple of approval went around the circle. The war chief called out to the women to bring more food.

"Take this news to your pony soldiers," the Badger leader told the scout. "The *Ihoka* will fight Wild Dog, for the sake of the Dakota. All we need do is meet and tell kill stories."

The women served food to the warriors; sweet buffalo hump from a kill made by Two Ponies. The leader of the Badger Lodge honored his guest by serving him first with the most succulent, golden fat-striped slices. The rebellious young men were forgotten, for now the lodge had come to a decision and would act accordingly. The feasting went on all night.

Eli left the next morning dead tired, his stomach achingly empty, despite the massive quantity of buffalo he had consumed. His head swam from lack of sleep. He was not so tired, however, that he missed the clear-cut wheel tracks on the trail back to where he left Andrews and the others. The wagons ran light, and Eli suspected it had to be the Baxter brothers. Brazen bastards, the scout thought as he swung away and followed the tracks for several miles. Shortly before noon, he came upon the Baxter camp.

Johnny sat by the fire, cooking a pan of beans.

"After tasting your brother's cooking I can see why

you do your own," Eli commented as he rode into the camp, his Winchester chambered and aimed at Johnny. The Baxter boy struggled to his feet.

"Well . . . h-hi there, Holten," he greeted, a smile scrambling for his lips. "Wha-what seems to be the problem? No need ta point your gun."

"Get your hands up, Baxter," Eli growled, still feeling the effects of the feast the night before. "I just had a long talk with a wise man and he says you've been selling guns to Wild Dog."

"Sell?" Johnny blurted. "Hell. Robbed is what he meant. I don't know why, but that renegade robbed us and let us go."

"Was that before or after the wagon train was wiped out?" Eli asked in a nasty tone of voice.

"Wa-wagon train?" Johnny stumbled, false confusion expertly painted on his face. "Why, I didn't hear about no wagon train."

"You and your brother are coming with me, Baxter," Eli growled. "And you're going to tell this to my lieutenant. With any kind of luck, you'll get to explain it all to the hangman, too."

Eli looked around the camp as his horse ambled a little closer to one of the tarp-covered wagons. Then he turned back to Johnny.

"Where is your brother, anyway?"

Bobby sprang out from under the tarp, an iron skillet in his hand. With all the strength he had, he cracked the metal across the back of Eli's head. The scout's hat softened the blow somewhat, but his Winchester discharged into the ground as he struggled to keep in his saddle. Bobby regained his balance on the wagon seat and delivered another thumping blow to the back of Holten's head. A burst of colored lights whirled the scout into darkness and he slid from the Morgan's back. Gleefully, Johnny got in a few solid kicks to the prone man's stomach and kidneys.

Bobby whooped and giggled as he leaped from the wagon, the skillet still in his grasp.

"Finally found a use for that thing," Johnny commented to Bobby, pointing at his brother's weapon.

"Boy," Bobby answered. "Won't Wild Dog be tickled with us? We're bringin' in Eli Holten."

Chapter Twelve

In any direction Sergeant Patrick Andrews looked, the gentle folds of the prairie stretched to the rim of the morning sky. The wild flowers of spring had faded away to leave browning buffalo grass swaying in the cool breezes of the heat to come.

Eli Holten was not in the picture, and he should have been. The apprehension Andrews experienced was not born entirely on behalf of the missing scout even though the non-com liked and admired Eli. There was also the fear that Two Ponies had laid a trap and was therefore hostile. That combined with the fact that he had permitted a fire to roast last night's pig dinner. He bitterly regretted that now, even though the scout had implied there was no risk by supplying the animal.

Christ, all he had to do was lose one man and there would be a court of inquiry, first, then a court martial due to that stinking pig he was still belching. No matter, even if the scout had ordered him to cook the lousy pig, the military responsibility was still his. Andrews fervently hoped if a man had to be lost from his tiny command, it would be himself. Just let it be quick, dear God.

"He shoulda' been here by now," Corporal Murphy volunteered.

"Bingo!" Andrews exploded testily. "Give that Rebel a blue uniform!"

"Well what the hail! Ah wuz jest say'n . . ."

"You'n your damn pig . . ."

"Mah pig? What the hail . . . Look Sahg, don' ya think Ahm worried, he's mah frien' too." Murphy got hold of himself. He took a deep breath and tried again. "All right, Sergeant. Where *is* Holten?"

"He told us to wait here, just in case it was a trap," the Scotsman said. "I'm figurin' that's what it's got to be. Although it doesn't make any sense."

A particularly deep rut bounced the wagon hard enough to wake the dead. It stirred Holten as well. He grunted in pain as he felt the dull throb in his head and the ropes that cut into his arms and legs.

"Hot diggety!" Bobby Baxter hooted. "Holten's coming around."

Obligingly Eli grunted again and struggled to understand where he was.

"Ya done yourself a favor, Holten." Johnny Baxter shouted over his shoulder, a toothy grin blinding in the morning sun. "Who knows what Wild Dog would have dreamt up to get you to come around." He laughed warmly, sincerity oozing from every pore in his well trained face. "As it is, old Wild Dog is gonna make the last day, or days, of your life so painful it hurts me to think about it."

"Why don't you just take some of that powerful medicine you've been feeding Wild Dog and go dream-walking with him?" the scout countered. "What is it, opium?"

Both boys' smiles twitched nervously as they glanced at each other.

"Looks like we got us a Pinkerton here, Bobby."

Johnny giggled self consciously. "Good thing he's gonna be dead soon."

"Not *too* soon if I know Wild Dog," Bobby added. Both boys laughed.

"I'll have you know, Mr. Holten," Johnny stated, "that all the young men of substance down in Atlanta use a little opium. It demonstrates a certain amount of decadence that the girls find attractive."

"How'd I get here?" Eli asked, his mind fading a bit with the pain.

"I smacked you one or two with my skillet!" Bobby answered.

"Umph, so you finally found a use for that thing?"

"Hey!" Bobby chirped happily. "That's what Johnny said!" He gave an especially big grin, then added. "We hid the other wagon, tied the horses to this one and headed for our favorite hostile's camp. You're gonna be a present, from us to him."

The sound of hoofbeats and the yipping of approaching warriors tensed Eli. The braves careened by, recklessly close to the wagon. Both Baxter boys flinched to the center of the seat.

"Hey fellers!" Johnny hooted nervously. "Hey! Look what we brung ya!" One brave glanced where the trader pointed and saw Eli Holten tied up in the back of the wagon. He shouted triumphantly and galloped away to spread the news. Tall Bear was a prisoner.

Another five minutes passed before the wagon rattled into the war camp of Wild Dog. Throughout that time, mounted warriors, painted for the warpath, had charged up to look at the prone scout in the bed of the half-covered buckboard. The commotion and noise in the camp seemed to disturb the Baxter boys more than it did Holten. Wild Dog had told them about how Holten had escaped from his camp once, embarrassing the medicine man in front of his braves,

139

and that he wanted the scout back. They had no idea how glad Wild Dog would be to see Holten again.

A beaming Wild Dog climbed over the backs of his braves to get to the wagon. He peered within and babbled hysterically in his chanting voice. Spittle ran from one corner of his mouth and his small, deep-set eyes glowed with an unholy fire.

"Get him to the fire," the howling leader commanded when he recovered himself.

A dozen hands reached in and dragged the struggling scout from the buckboard, while ten times that many braves vied for an opportunity to strike or spit upon the captive. Wild Dog danced around the throng to his own, unheard music, his chant growing ever louder and faster. Some of the warriors also chanted, Wild Dog's insanity writhing only across their faces, not yet imbedded in their hearts.

Eli fell hard next to a fire that crackled warmly in the morning air. The jubilant ring closed in around him.

"Wild Dog," Johnny Baxter announced as he approached the fire and stood before the war chief. "We bring you this gift because of our deep respect for you. Also, I would like to give you these things we took from Holten."

Bobby lumbered up with Sonny, Eli's horse. All of the scout's weapons hung from the saddle. Wild Dog circled to the right of the animal at a respectable distance, as though it constituted a great mystery. Silent for once, he appraised the gift appreciatively. At last he grunted and nodded vigorously. "It is a good horse. Good weapons. I will ride this horse and use this rifle in the next raid we make."

Both Baxter brothers smiled and nodded back while the medicine man's followers shouted their approval. When quiet returned, Wild Dog looked down scornfully at the prisoner.

"So, Tall Bear," he growled menacingly as he approached Holten, the hated symbol of the white man soldiers. "You have decided to visit us again."

"If I am not welcome, I will move on," Eli answered blandly, trying to clear his head.

"But you *are* welcome," Wild Dog sang out and put his face an inch away from Eli's. "You must pay for the honor of being here, but you are welcome."

Wild Dog straightened and threw his hands above his head to command silence again. "Hear me, oh warriors of the song," he shouted as he stepped between the fire and their prisoner. "I wish to speak to all . . . and especially to Tall Bear." All the frenzy in Wild Dog's face concentrated into his eyes and his voice echoed powerfully so that even the most distant could hear.

"I knew since I was a small boy that I was chosen to rid the land of the whites. My family was murdered by the whites . . ."

A lie, Holten knew, yet he found himself fascinated and listened carefully to Wild Dog's version of his holy mission. "Yet, they spared me," the unbalanced medicine man went on. "When I was twelve I fasted for many days, only eating peyote buds and the rank weed that grows along the creeks. This brought me a dream that made me see a powerful song, one so filled with kill stories that I knew it had a verse for every white on the land. I will sing my song over Tall Bear, the pretend Oglala who is white and lives with the whites, as we see how he takes pain until he dies."

A sweet, gentle smile overtook the war leader's face. He studied his victim with a look that should have been reserved for wives. "It will be a very . . . long . . . song, Tall Bear," he said softly.

"Whoooeee!" Bobby enthused. "Johnny, you catch

141

that? Just like we said. Long, long song." The younger Baxter boy chortled happily.

"We got some other news for you, Wild Dog," Johnny added soberly in a quiet moment. "Seems the Army is out again roundin' up all the settlers that didn' come in the first time and takin' 'em over to Fort Rawlins." The corrupt trader waggled a finger at the medicine man. "Cain't do business unless ya got somethin' to trade with, Wild Dog."

"They are again on our land?" Wild Dog pondered, his eyes lost in concentration. "I had not heard this. They take the whites where we are still too few to attack. And if I cannot gather victories and scalps, no more warriors will join me. The ones I have will grow bored with my war. I must stop this."

"You mean attack the Cavalry?" Bobby asked.

"Why not?" Johnny answered for the deranged medicine chief. "He's got enough men to wipe out . . . Hey, Holten, how many troopers are there gathering up all these settlers?"

The scout made an obscene gesture in sign language that Johnny didn't understand. The assembled warriors did and chuckled at it.

"If I were to destroy these Long Knives that gather the ground diggers together, I would have many more braves join me," Wild Dog speculated aloud to the sky. He whirled and pointed a finger at the two white traders.

"You will go to find these Long Knives," he ordered. "As you did with the rolling wood lodges before, you will find out how many guns and how much gold there is with them. Once you have this, you will return and we will fall upon them and slaughter every one. I have spoken."

Both Baxters smiled ear to ear, a dazzling display of ivory.

"Go now," Wild Dog commanded.

"Take it real slow with ol' Holten here, won't ya?" Bobby pleaded. "I sorta wanna watch a little when we get back. I ain't never seen someone get tortured to death befo'e."

"C'mon, Bobby, we gotta go," Johnny urged as he headed for the wagon. "We'll take on'y two spare horses."

"Hey, Johnny," Bobby called, excited with his grand idea. "If we make enough money off this, we could go home and buy back the brewery."

"No!" the elder brother snapped.

"Aw, c'mon, Johnny," Bobby whined. "It's been in our family for generations."

"I said no. We do that an' we're liable to git lynched," Holten heard him exclaim as the warriors tightened the ring around the scout, eyes alight with expectation.

Chapter Thirteen

Like savages themselves, the two Baxter boys whooped out of the renegade camp, waving their hats like flags over their heads. They left the scout behind for the games of the drug-demented Wild Dog and his men.

"What would be the right way to start on you, Tall Bear?" Wild Dog speculated, then answered his own question. "We should do homage to the powers of the earth."

He walked to the fire and removed a long piece of wood that had recently been inserted. One end burned brightly. Without a moment's hesitation, he plunged it against Eli's buckskin shirt. The leather didn't catch, but the heat seared through to Holten's chest.

The scout didn't flinch, nor show any signs of discomfort, although he felt hairs on his chest shrivel from the heat. Wild Dog pulled the brand away and studied the white man soberly.

"Pull his clothes off," the leader of the renegades ordered.

Immediately two braves grabbed Eli, cut his bonds and dragged off his fringed shirt and buckskin trousers. A little ripple of appreciation ran through the crowd at the sight of his exposed male member.

No wonder the women liked Tall Bear so well, was the consensus. Swiftly they retied his arms and legs with rawhide thongs. Wild Dog nodded approval and directed a young brave to continue the torturing so he would be free to start singing again. Covertly he slid a ball of sticky brown sap-oozing opium into his mouth.

"Hold coals in his armpits until he screams out for mercy," Wild Dog ordered. "You two, erect two poles with a cross-bar so we can stand him up for arrow practice later on."

The camp's residents crowded around to watch. Like children burning an ant hill, they looked on avidly, while the chant of Wild Dog's dementia spread through the ranks that watched with glazed eyes and added to their savor of the scene.

"Why do you follow this outcast?" Eli yelled out before the brave could start his torture. "He has powerful magic . . . but it comes from that pouch at his waist. He is not even true to the words of his song. He says he hates all whites, yet he keeps two white men close to his side. What does this mean?"

A low rumble passed through the crowd watching. Many had been bothered by the Baxter brothers' presence. To themselves they wondered why these two should be so differently handled than all other whites Wild Dog chanced upon.

"What whites do I keep at my side?" the leader asked, interrupting his incessant song. Then, again, answered his own question. "Do you mean the two traders who have teeth that glow?" Wild Dog laughed warmly, his twisted smile writhing like the demon in his eyes.

"Next time you see them, look at their skin closely. They are not white! They are black men, like those the White Grandfather in Wash-ing-ton released. They only pretend to be white. This they have confided to me. Once there are no more whites on the land, they will fade away like the morning mist under the hot sun. For they are nothing but black spirits in white men's shadows. So weak are the whites that they cannot hold on to their own sun-casts."

Laughter rippled through the gathered warriors. Some because they found it so funny that whites could not keep their own shadows, others because they thought their leader had told a funny story. Either way, they no longer listened to Eli. The scout realized these braves had as yet to fight the Buffalo Soldiers of the Tenth and Fourth Cavalry, the all-colored regiments with their white officers. They'd probably never seen a Negro. They wouldn't know what a real one looked like. Clever of Wild Dog to play on this ignorance; he gave the mystic credit. With the tension released, thought now was given to the torture of the scout.

His arms cut free from the thongs, willing hands stretched them out to make small pits for the embers. A hot brand was brought from the fire, then the young warrior that Wild Dog had chosen gingerly applied the flaming white coal under Eli's arms with a pair of tongs taken from a settler's ranch.

Pain seared through Eli Holten's body, the smell of his own flesh burning rankled his nose, yet he dared not show any discomfort or cry out. If he did, nothing he said would be respected.

Many among the throng sighed and grunted in admiration of the white man's endurance as the young warrior pulled the fading ember away. Wild Dog barely watched, his eyes glazed and distant as he sang out clearly.

The pain stayed and Eli knew he couldn't hope to survive for long. Desperately he called out at the chanting war chief.

"Could you take this pain, Wild Dog?" he challenged. "I am brave, strong and fearless. Why should I be killed and a mongrel dog with flecks of foam in its mouth be allowed to lead?"

Ecstasy glowed on Wild Dog's face like a beacon. Ignoring Holten, he lustily continued his song. Eli feared the madman's frenzy prevented him from hearing and his desperation grew.

"I have never seen you fight, Wild Dog," Holten taunted as the next tongful of ember was hoisted to the other side of his chest. The scout bit his lower lip to remain silent while the fiery matter ate at his flesh, the sensitive nerves under his arm shrieking in agony at the unflinching body which lay and took the assault.

"When we last met, you stood and sang as you do now, leaving the work of men to men," Holten continued when the misery subsided. "Could it be that you are a woman? Or a contrary? Perhaps your fury toward whites comes from lying about your manhood vision. I say you reached for the browstrap instead of the bowstring!"

Shock at this insult became a deadly rumble among Wild Dog's followers. Wild Dog still seemed oblivious. He had begun to rock on his heels as he chanted. His death-summoning prayers left a twisted smile on his face. Globs of spittle began to foam at the corners of his mouth.

Soon, Eli knew, the agony would become too great, he would cry out in pain.

"If Wild Dog had fought the last time we met, perhaps I would not have escaped to leave many men dead or dying behind me. Perhaps he is a coward when faced with the likes of me . . . a real man."

The deadly, multi-level insult, questioning his masculinity, implying cowardice and suggesting that

Wild Dog was not an Indian, but some sort of non-person, seemed not to affect the chanting medicine chief. The new set of embers burned closer up in his arm pit and Eli's scream could only be held back by biting his tongue. When at last he could continue to speak, the scout gasped out the words.

"And what about your song, Wild Dog? Isn't it true that the so-called mighty medicine song comes to you only when you eat the little balls that Johnny Baxter gives you?"

"No!" Wild Dog screamed, jerked out of his trance. "The song is with me always. It is all I see and all I feel."

"You say I am a white man, though the Baxters are not," Eli pressed. "Well, if I'm white, then I ought to know another white man . . . and I say that the Baxters are white. Could they have given Wild Dog a false song? Or perhaps the dream-walking only reveals Wild Dog's own death song. Perhaps the coward that is Wild Dog dares not die alone and wants to take all these brave warriors with him, to protect him in the Hunting Grounds."

"You cannot say such lies, white man," Wild Dog shouted as he drew nearer to the scout.

"I speak only the truth. If my words offend you, then prove I lie by showing you are braver, that your song can kill. Release me and fight me."

"I need prove nothing," Wild Dog countered. A disapproving rumble went through the crowd. Not so loud as he would wish, Eli thought, but far more than Wild Dog expected. Wild Dog looked around and knew he had to do something. He pointed an accusing finger at his tormentor.

"For these words you will die. *You* shall be proven the coward and liar."

"Then release me and give me my knife. I will kill

you with it. Or is it true that the only balls you have are those given you by the Baxters?"

Stung beyond endurance or careful reason, Wild Dog made an abrupt sign. The rawhide thongs were cut from Eli's wrists. The young warrior who had done the burning now ran to Eli's Morgan and pulled the Bowie knife from its sheath. He walked back, holding the blade aloft like a religious relic.

Though the fire still burned in his chest and his fingers barely functioned from being tied so long, Eli felt jubilation. If he could kill Wild Dog, it would end the whole uprising. All he need do was best the medicine man in honest combat. What more could he ask for?

The malignant cleverness in Wild Dog's eyes had not faded. He darted a glance around the ring of warriors as Holten retrieved his knife and a clearing formed for the fight. A slow smile creased Wild Dog's full lips. He threw his arms in the air and cried to his followers.

"My song will kill the white man." With his chin he pointed to a tall, thick warrior who towered over the other braves. "Young Elk," Wild Dog shouted. The brave stepped through the crowd to stand before his leader.

"Do you think I am a coward?" Wild Dog demanded.

"No, Wild Dog," the simple-minded Young Elk answered. "The white man lies. You are more brave than any man. Your song fills me with strength."

"Then . . . I will sing," Wild Dog shouted, ". . . and you . . . will kill the liar."

Eli's heart sank. The wily madman had chosen a champion. Anger coursed in liquid fire through his veins.

"I want to fight you," the scout shouted at Wild Dog.

149

"You will die in the grip of my song," the crafty fanatic answered.

"I will win . . . and then die by treachery," Eli countered. "You dare not face or release a truly brave man. Your heart is as yellow as the piss my horse spills on the ground."

Wild Dog winced at the insult and looked up at the towering warrior, Tall Bear, who boasted many scalps and had killed often with the knife he grasped in his hand.

"If you win," Wild Dog pronounced slowly," I will give you back your horse and your guns and let you ride out of this camp. That is how sure I am of your death."

Holten took a long look at the huge man in breech-cloth who stood before him like a mountain. Wild Dog's champion had more muscle than most men had bodies. The scout swallowed hard and nodded.

"Let it begin. I will win and then ride out," Eli agreed.

"You will die and I will scalp you," Young Elk spoke to Holten.

No doubt about it, Eli thought. He was in trouble.

Andrews, Murphy and the three extra men rode at full speed to the head of the column. Estillman gave them an offhand, indifferent salute, his nose buried in Deborah's letter. Sgt. Andrews bit off a favorite caustic remark non-coms reserved for mooning troopers that nearly jumped to his lips as the morose lieutenant somberly looked up from his letter.

"The lieutenant's permission, sir, and I wish to report, sir," Sgt. Pat Andrews declared with a salute.

"Where's Mr. Holten, Sergeant?" Estillman demanded.

"That's what I'm reportin', sir," Andrews stated. "He went to Two Ponies' camp and he had us wait a few miles away so the Injuns wouldn't know we were there. Just in case it might be a trap, you see, sir. The scout never showed up again. We looked all over for him without actually goin' into the camp. He told us to report to you if he didn't come back and tell you that you're on your own."

Estillman absently folded the letter and stuck it over his heart as he stared out across the rolling landscape of the prairie. "It seems to me that they went to an awful lot of trouble to capture one man. What do you think, Sergeant Morrison?" he inquired of the first sergeant.

"Well, it might be presumptuous o' me ta hazard a guess, sir. Me just bein' the first sergeant . . ."

"I value your opinion, First Sergeant Morrison," Estillman interrupted. "Besides, the only other person in this column that out-ranks you is Lt. Leary."

Both men looked in unison over at the nervous shavetail who rode behind one of the settlers' wagons, anxiously scanning the horizon. They glanced knowingly at each other.

Morrison cleared his throat. "I think yer right, Lieutenant," he agreed. "A frightful lot of trouble for one man. Besides, the scout wouldn't a gone in if he *thought* it was a trap. From what Andrews said, he left 'em outside as a precaution, so's to speak."

"So, what happened to Eli Holten?" the lieutenant persisted.

"If it's foul play, sir, only God and Eli's own wits are gonna get the scout outta it," Morrison answered. "And I'm not too proud a man ta pray far him a little."

151

Young Elk lunged and Eli marveled at the speed of such a large man as the scout tried to evade the brave's knife. The blade nicked his chest and a new pain joined the burns.

Holten wheeled around and punched Young Elk in the side of his face as the brave leaned into another thrust. It felt like punching a cottonwood. Eli reversed and slashed under the tall man's arms. The knife slid across the warrior's chest as Young Elk leaped backward. A move that Eli had killed with before got at best a little trickle of blood from the huge brave.

The audience howled after the first unexpected lunge by Wild Dog's champion. Now they shouted encouragement indiscriminately as the two combatants cautiously circled each other.

Young Elk feinted time and again, used his greater arm length to force Eli to charge deeply into his range. Wild Dog stood nearby, seemingly oblivious to the fight. His eyes had turned to the sky and the disjoined words of his song spilled from his slack mouth.

Another sizzling attack by Young Elk left the brave open to a left-handed jab by Holten. It landed harmlessly against the warrior's shoulders. The burly Yankton Sioux grunted with the power he placed behind the blow. If he'd thrust relaxed and fast he would have buried it up to the hilt in Eli's chest. Instead the scout whirled and smacked his enemy again, a solid thump to the head with his elbow. He danced away as Young Elk shook off the effects and lunged again. Eli blocked and his Bowie slit flesh on the inside of Young Elk's left forearm. Nothing seemed to bother the big moose, Eli thought. He did take note that the huge man always thrust, never slashed with his blade. Crouched, Holten worked closer to his opponent, who feinted and stabbed at the

152

air that separated the two men.

Holten tired rapidly, pulled down by exhaustion, blood loss and torture. He blinked his eyes, an almost fatal mistake! Young Elk thrust at him again and he only escaped death by a fraction of an inch. Eli forced himself to dodge under the blow and go to the inside to make a wild slash at Young Elk's chest.

This time the blade dug deeply below the brave's left nipple and cut a long trough through the pectoral muscle. Young Elk seemed unshaken by the blood-streaming slash as he wheeled back and delivered a solid smash with the hilt of the knife in his right hand. The power of his body weight and twist of his wrist slammed the scout at the base of his neck. It sent sparks through the sudden blackness before Holten's eyes as he tumbled forward.

Eli landed on his shoulder and rolled over once, then a second time as he gained distance from danger and recovered his sight. What he saw sank his heart another foot into the ground. Young Elk stood firm and tall, blood washing down across the whole of his torso, yet apparently unbothered as he went into a panther crouch and threw himself at the scout with a strident war cry on his lips.

Again Eli rolled, this time into Young Elk's legs, throwing the brave to the ground. Holten turned quickly, though not before the warrior had recovered his defense. Young Elk lay on the ground with one hand pushing him upward and the other slashing with the knife. Eli fell back, got to his feet and settled into a solid crouch.

Young Elk rose from the ground with a contemptuous grin on his face. "This white man is boring sport," he said and threw the knife away. "Wild Dog. Give me an arrow. I will drive it through his heart with my bare hand and save my knife for his scalp."

"An arrow!" Eli jeered. "You are a child, Young Elk. An old woman." He threw away his knife. "Wild Dog. Give me a bowstring."

Young Elk looked confused, then nodded, determined to best the scout. "Then I will take a bowstring."

Braves near the combatants retrieved the knives and now provided bowstrings made of buffalo sinew. Thrown from the sidelines, they landed at each fighter's feet. Eli quickly inspected the loops at each end of the stout, pliable material. Young Elk, uncertain of this strange form of combat, wrapped the string tightly around his right fist and slipped the two loops over his thumb to bind the striking surface tightly.

"I will kill you with this, Tall Bear," Young Elk bragged and shook his fist at the scout. Good, Holten thought. Few Indians knew how to throw punches. Their bare-hand fighting consisted mostly of slaps, grapples and kicks. Holten bent low and took up a short, stout piece of twig that fit nearly in his palm. He slipped a loop over it as the young warrior suddenly lunged at him.

Eli also lunged, threw himself at the warrior's feet, rolled over on his back and kicked up into Young Elk's chest.

It was like kicking a mossy rock. Young Elk grunted and fell back as if he'd bounced off an invisible wall. Eli came back to his feet with another piece of wood in his hand. It broke as he put pressure on it. Holten threw the chips in Young Elk's face as the brave charged again. The young man showed no reaction to the wood as he hauled off and slapped Eli alongside the head.

The scout saw a moment of black and doubled over. Young Elk shot a knee to Holten's face, split his

154

lip and snapped him off his feet. Dazed, Holten lay in the dust.

Young Elk screamed his war cry as he fell toward the prone scout. Eli rolled to his left and snapped a grazing left hook across one of Young Elk's wounds. His other hand frantically scrabbled on the ground.

Eli came up with another piece of wood. It didn't yield to his crushing fist. The other loop slipped over this piece. Eli formed a wide circle with the bow string, wrists crossed. He staggered, feigning greater weakness than he felt, as he regained his footing. A queasiness boiled in his throat as he thought of what he must do. Young Elk confidently closed with bare hands raised, faked with his tightly wrapped one, then threw a low gut swipe with the other.

It connected and the breath wheezed out of Holten as he stepped inside Young Elk's grasp, his wrists still crossed. Young Elk's string-wrapped hand scraped along Eli's jawline as the scout slipped up the outside of the warrior's other arm, then dropped the looped bow string over Young Elk's head.

Eli jerked his wrists apart with every ounce of strength he could summon as he landed behind Young Elk's back. The improvised garotte snapped across the hulking warrior's throat like `a band of steel. Eli pivoted under his upraised arms and bent double. His motion hoisted Young Elk off the ground.

Young Elk made a gurgling sound as he hung suspended between earth and sky, the painful bite of the strangling cord cut off his air and his eyes bulged. His fingers rose jerkily and dug for the bowstring now buried in his flesh. His tongue, already blackening, protruded from his distorted mouth. He drummed his heels and his legs jarred his captor, though Eli hung on with all his might. The body gave a powerful lurch and Young Elk released his bowels. Urine dumped to the ground and he went slack.

Eli released the string and the corpse slid from his back, leaving a trail of ordure, and plopped on the ground.

A long moment's silence slipped by as everyone present stared gape-mouthed at the unmoving warrior. Wild Dog abruptly stopped singing and blinked uncomprehendingly at his dead champion. A chorus of awed voices rose from the crowd.

Eli fell backward from exhaustion and landed on his buttocks, his chest heaving and his tongue hanging out like a panting dog. The burns and bloody wound made his head swirl for a moment and he struggled to stay conscious. His knife fell next to him from the hand of the brave who had taken it. Holten absently picked it up and struggled to his feet.

"Hear me," he shouted. "Wild Dog's song is not so powerful that I could not defeat it. He cannot overcome the Long Knives with his song." Eli turned to the medicine man and thrust his chin at him. "You said you would give me my horse and weapons back and let me ride out of here. I call on that promise now."

Wild Dog stared past the scout to where Young Elk lay, twisted by the onset of his death throes.

"But I am a coward, Tall Bear," Wild Dog purred. "A coward and a liar. You said so. Surely such a man would kill you and put you to the flame."

A mutter of disapproval went through the braves. A young warrior had brought Eli's horse to Wild Dog. He looked apprehensively from one powerful man to the other.

"If I am afraid of you, I could not let you leave. If I am a liar, my promise is worth nothing."

Eli tensed. He glanced out of the corner of his eye, looking for an escape route. Even if he got out of the camp, his wounds and weakness could kill him before he reached safety. But first, he could kill Wild Dog.

The unhinged war leader also glanced around. He could see his warriors had been impressed by this white man. If he did not keep his word, they would desert him. Wild Dog pushed the warrior holding the Morgan toward Eli.

"Take your horse, Tall Bear," he growled. "Take it and ride. I am Wild Dog and I am not afraid of you or any white man."

Once again Eli glanced around. An opening had formed where the Baxters had brought him in and where their wagon now waited. Along it, warriors stood with their crow-wing fans, waving them in a sign of respect. He struggled to the back of his horse, weakness and nausea surging over him in waves. He straightened up, touched heels to Sonny's flanks and rode off.

"Hau-hau! Hau-hau!" rose a chorus of approval as the scout moved along the living corridor to freedom.

Chapter Fourteen

His burns went deep and the skin looked like something Bobby Baxter had cooked. Eli directed his horse to a small creek and traveled upstream a mile before finding a place where he could tend to his wounds. For the time being, all Holten wanted to do was wash the burns and stop the bleeding. He felt better simply by being out of Wild Dog's camp. Once more he had lost much blood and failed to kill the deranged fanatic. For the sake of Black Spotted Horse, Gray Otter and the others, he had to get vengeance. He found a likely spot and slid from Sonny's back.

Eli had stopped once on the way to cut leaves from a cactus in the aloe family. Now, after washing his wounds with painful thoroughness he smeared them with the syrupy pulp and packed wet moss over them. The pain began to ease and he tackled the shallow, bloody slash on his chest.

After he bound it with a long strip of gauze from his saddle bag, he replaced everything. His stomach growled, reminding him he had not eaten all day. No more time could be wasted, though. Holten loaded his gear back onto Sonny, then dragged himself into the saddle. He pointed the Morgan's nose in the proper direction and headed for where he figured the relief column had to be. The scout hoped fervently that the

Baxter brothers would still be with the troopers.

"Saints preserve us!" Morrison shouted as he saw the scout approaching. The first sergeant turned his horse and trotted back toward Eli Holten. "I'd given ye up fur dead, lad," he blurted, eyes misting. A little closer and the Irishman's paternal concern etched into his face. "Holten, lad! Ye've been terrible wounded."

With bumbling tenderness, the sergeant escorted Eli to a settler's wagon where medical supplies had been stored. Estillman had halted the column for the night although two hours of daylight remained. The settlers tired quickly and the animals needed feed and water. Soldiers and civilians came running when they saw the wounded man.

The scout's body twisted with the discomfort of his new sores. Morrison dismounted and carefully eased the wounded man from his horse. Then he helped him walk the few paces to the wagon where Helga Brunnen set about recleaning his wounds. Estillman approached the Conestoga and leaned over Helga's ample frame to see the scout.

"Report, Mr. Holten," the officer ordered.

Without hesitation, though Helga's searing look could have killed the young lieutenant, Eli began to explain the meeting he had with Two Ponies, the agreement they reached about Wild Dog.

"If it all went so cozy, Scout, what happened to you?"

"I got bushwhacked by Johnny and Bobby Baxter," Eli explained. "Two Ponies told me they've been supplying Wild Dog with guns, whiskey . . . and opium, of all things." He described the torture and combat at Wild Dog's camp. Then concluded. "According to Two Ponies, it's possible that the

Baxter brothers set up the wagon train. When they get here I want to have a nice little talk with them."

Estillman scowled. "They've already been here, Mr. Holten. Very helpful Southern gentlemen. After asking us about what was going on they headed out. Said they knew about a group of new settlers that had only arrived and were building homesteads over to the north. They went to round them up for us."

Eli looked up at the young officer. "Lieutenant, we could be attacked at any moment."

"First Sergeant," Estillman calmly ordered. "There's a small bluff with a clump of trees and good clear ground around it back about a mile. Remember it?"

"Aye, sir, and a beautiful place it'd be far settin' up a defense, especially since there's a good-sized creek runnin' to the back of it."

"Then get the wagons moving at once. We have no time."

Morrison's voice bellowed out. The alert ran through the homesteaders like a fire in the prairie grass. Rifles came out and horses were quickly rehitched. It took fifteen minutes. By that time, outriders began to report a sudden flurry of activity by Indians nearby.

"Mr. Holten," Estillman inquired as he watched the last wagon swing into line and E Troop start leading the anxious civilians back the way they came. "How are you feeling?"

"Much better now that I'm patched up right proper," Eli answered.

"Are you strong enough to go get us some help from the fort?"

Eli looked to the east. It appeared clear enough. Most of the flanking screens had reported hostiles to the north and west. "I surely better try. I can tell you right now, Lieutenant, the way those Baxter boys were talking, they mean to get this column massacred. I could do with something to eat, first. Anything I can take along and chew on in the saddle will do."

Estillman nodded, then without another word, rode off. Helga sniffed and set her jaw as her eyes coldly followed the officer's exit. Eli noted the change in her attitude.

"You mad at the lieutenant, Miss Brunnen?" Eli asked as she finished the final bandage on his chest.

"He broke mine heart vonce, he shall not break it again," she intoned dramatically, then left for the front of the wagon.

Eli ate a hasty meal of sausage, bread and a cup of coffee, provided by the Brunnen larder. It only partly filled his stomach; he headed up to the supply wagon. He planned to ride all night and reach the fort by mid-day following.

"You'll hurry, won't ya, Scout," Warren Murphy asked as Eli rechecked his weapons and extra ammunition in his saddle bags. "I sure would like better company than the likes of Michael Delehanty Morrison for when I die."

"You could do worse," Eli countered as he hoisted himself back into the saddle. The first sergeant, he observed, had overheard Murphy's remarks and now boiled in their direction.

"Ain't it a shame ye should be so picky about the company ye keep," Morrison said as he closed in on the supply wagon. "Typical it is of ye Ulster-Orangemen to be thinkin' yer better than most. Watch yer clever lip, me bucko, or ye're likely to find it doobled in size."

Murphy laughed. "Ya know, Sergeant, sooner or later, I'm gonna belt ye a good one."

"Oh, ye're quite the destroyer, ye are, ain'cha,

Murphy, me lad. Best be savin' all that terrifying strength far Wild Dog an' his heathens, don't ye think?"

Murphy sobered. "Yes, First Sergeant. Good luck, Mr. Holten."

"I'll get the general to send the whole regiment if need be."

Eli touched spurs to Sonny's flanks and the powerful animal surged forward.

His wounds still hurt, he could have used some sleep and he was still hungry. Nonetheless, he checked his bearings one more time, studied the short-cut he planned to take on his mental map and swung away from the trail.

The bluff was really no more than a rise, though scrubby bushes struggled at the base of the rolling ground. They provided a natural barrier some fifty yards from where the prairie grass ended and the cottonwoods above offered some cover. Exactly where Morrison had said, Estillman found a sluggish, but fairly wide, stream ambling out past the south side of the rise, the waterway swinging up from the west, then headed southeast from there.

"If it pleases the lieutenant," Morrison reported. "We're puttin' the wagons at the base of them trees, sir, for a little more coverage. They still form somethin' of a circle all the way except for this part back here."

"Make sure to put picket posts back here, First Sergeant," Estillman suggested. "Perhaps you can use some of the civilians. Where's Lt. Leary?"

"Out findin' out what the civilians have in the way of weapons, sir," the Irish NCO explained. "This group's not nearly as well armed as that first bunch we brought in."

162

"The ones least willing to cooperate with the Army are the ones least prepared to defend themselves." Estillman paused. "Does that make sense?"

"No, sir," Morrison answered honestly. "But at least it's consistent."

Eli ran Sonny hard for the first few minutes, then warily decided to proceed at a walk and study the trail. He'd noticed unshod hoofprints a few feet into the brush when he went for water, now he sensed the presence of the renegades. Finally convinced some of Wild Dog's people were ahead, he mounted a bluff, climbed a tree and, with his field glasses, studied the ground ahead.

Thin plumes of dust sprouted over the rolling terrain to the east. Wild Dog's numbers must have swollen and these, Eli observed, had headed west, directly toward him. He could see some movement of horses both to the north and south. Probably scouts looking for someone attempting to do what he was doing. Wild Dog didn't want reinforcements for the relief column. The crazed war leader intended to have a clear-cut beauty of a massacre to gather even more hot-heads to his cause. The scout knew he couldn't hope to slip through. Besides, an alternative he had detected looked quite appealing.

Holten shinnied down the tree and repacked his field glasses, then contemplated his new route. He would have no time to go back to the column to let Estillman know what he had in mind. Two Ponies' camp seemed closer than the fort anyway. At least Wild Dog wouldn't be looking for anyone going that direction for help. If Two Ponies wanted to stop Wild Dog, this would be his last chance. Once Wild Dog managed to wipe out a troop of cavalry and twenty wagons of settlers, there'd be all-out war. No one would bother to ask if one band happened to be good Indians or bad when they got set to shoot them.

In the next instant, the scout heard sporadic explosions of rifle fire and he knew he had to hurry.

"We're being attacked!" Abner Leary screamed at Estillman, who had started down the hill. This time, Loren noted smugly, it was the junior officer whose voice broke.

Sure enough, a wave of Sioux, Asiniboine and a smattering of several other plains tribes came screaming their blood-lust as their mounts ate up the distance between the grass to the north and the wagons to the south. As Estillman took in the situation, return fire started.

"Looks like you're right, Mister Leary," Estillman answered soberly.

Chapter Fifteen

Although he ran downhill, Lt. Estillman looked strangely peaceful, as though concentrating on a game of chess or some complex tactical problem in a classroom at West Point. He never took his eyes off the charging enemy as he pulled his Colt. Wild Dog's followers raced out of the cover of a gulch no more than two hundred yards away. Surprise had eaten up half that distance.

"Cease firing!" Estillman shouted, his voice breaking on the command. "All civilians back to the trees."

"Back to the trees, the lot of ye," Morrison repeated as he pushed one hesitant settler toward the nearby cottonwoods to emphasize his point.

"We're gonna need every gun we got, Loren," Lt. Leary bleated. "Why are you ordering them back?"

"Because when those Indians get to within fifty yards of us, we're going to fire by volleys," Estillman patiently explained. Morrison immediately assumed the order.

"Platoon Sergeants! Prepare for volley fire! First rank kneel . . . second rank, offhand."

"The civilians are panicked and undisciplined," Estillman continued, completely in his element. "They'll fire wildly, spook our troopers and ruin that volley."

The howling warriors ate up the ground, firing randomly at the row of wagons.

"Prepare to fire, First Sergeant," the troop commander told Morrison softly.

"Troop . . . Prepare to load . . . Load."

The next order came from the leathery lungs of the three platoon sergeants. "Take aim . . ."

The wall of dust the wild braves stirred into life made them look like one brown, irresistible monster, wallowing off the prairie, that came to engulf the thin blue line of troops in its choking miasma. Although sixty yards still separated the company of pony soldiers from the overwhelming wave of screaming warriors, it felt like the boiling mass had already over-run the wagons. The ground vibrated ceaselessly from the pounding of nearly four hundred hoofs.

"We'll bring out the settlers when we go to individual fire," Estillman explained softly to his subordinate officer, who loomed over him. Loren turned and looked up. "And . . . Abner," he continued in a quiet, icy tone. "Don't *ever* again question an order I give."

Right then, Abner Leary wished most heartily that he could be in that nice office in Supply Depot in Columbus, Ohio, at the recruiting center there. It was, after all, what had been promised to him. How had he managed to wind up in the Cavalry? Worse, to find himself under the command of "Squeaky" Estillman, only one class his senior at the Point. It had been so carefully planned. Then to be trapped in a place like this . . . with all of those . . . *hostiles* out there actually trying to kill him. He felt a trembling in his chest and just *knew* it was a heart seizure. Why, there weren't even any girls out on this forsaken prairie. No cotillions, no balls, no formal dinners or dress parades. In fact, none of the reasons for wanting to be an officer and gentlemen. A nervous titter started up in Abner's throat. Whatever had possessed him to pursue a military career? His father, of course, and Senator Grimes.

"Only people of the proper class should fill the ranks of our officer corps," his father had often pontificated. And Senator Grimes had echoed that sentiment. And . . . Abner Leary, son of a multi-millionaire railroad executive, found himself on the frontier, facing a horde of screaming savages.

"Is that clear, Abner?" Estillman demanded.

"Yes, Loren . . . er, sir."

Wild Dog's death-cloud seemed to howl above them, a dust devil with the power of a tornado come to suck the very breath from their lungs. Yet, the troopers held their fire, discipline binding them to their officer's orders, desperation grappling with their pounding hearts.

"Fire!" Estillman shouted as the warriors crossed his calculated fifty yard line.

"Fire, lads! Fire," Morrison echoed.

The platoon sergeants took up the drill. "Give . . . Fire! . . . Reload! . . . Second rank . . . Aim! . . . Fire!"

A counter-cloud formed suddenly over the wagons, made of the greasy, gray-white smoke from black powder. The first rank of charging horses collapsed as the beasts and warriors hit a wall of hot lead. Dead and wounded men bolted over the top of the shot-up animals' heads and fell heavily to plow the hard ground with their teeth. The tide that the downed braves had been a part of mercilessly boiled over them. The first rank fired again.

Carbines cranked open, expended casings ejected from the single-shot government issue weapons and troopers' nimble fingers re-loaded them on command.

"Take aim! . . . Fire!" Morrison yelled along with his sergeants, long before the troopers could reload. He had to. The warriors even now closed within ten yards. Those soldiers who were ready burst a fourth volley into the chests of the animals so quickly close at hand. Another row of horses suddenly lost their front feet, plummeting to the earth, their riders cartwheeling over the heads of the mounts. They suffered the fate of the earlier victims of the deadly volley fire. Some of the braves didn't land on the ground. They bounced off wheels and the hard wood walls of the wagons.

This time the charge broke. Ponies split irregularly to the east and west, the energy of the attack expended. Freed for targets of opportunity, soldiers chose their aim at close range now. Estillman raised his Colt and fired a shot at the rows of warriors who ran past like clay pigeons. He hooted with excitement at the smoke and confusion that washed over the scene of mayhem.

"Wasn't that great?" Estillman shouted at Leary.

"I'm scared shitless," Leary wailed back, his face pale and drawn.

"Well . . . that, too," Estillman admitted. "Time to get your civilians in action."

Most had come running the moment the seemingly irresistible wall of warriors had been split. They fired rifles and shotguns at the swirling mass of targets that danced out past the line of wagons.

Targeting went both ways. A trooper screamed out as a slug bit through his scalp, tearing at the side of his head and blowing blood in a fine spray. One of the platoon sergeants hoisted himself across the back of a wagon as he scrambled for better cover. Before he could make it, an arrowhead burst through the front of his shirt as the fletchings stopped the shaft in his back. A sodbuster crawled under one wagon to snipe from the ground. Then he screamed in agony when a howling warrior stuck a war lance in his left eye.

Wild Dog watched from the ridge of the gulley where the attack had started. A pair of field glasses Johnny Baxter had given him let him see the battle better. It seemed like a good attack.

Wild Dog and his followers had the power of surprise on their side. The gulley had been deep enough for the warriors to walk their animals in without being noticed. The soldiers recovered quickly, though, and Wild Dog could see a hard fight ahead. If they had caught the pony soldiers and the white men out in the open, he mused, where the Baxters told him they were, his men would have had quick, easy kills. The first charge had been turned. It didn't matter, Wild Dog thought as he began to chant his song aloud. It would grind down to a war of attrition. He had men he'd held back to send in fresh on the second wave, and a third if needed. The whites fought with all they had. And he had made sure no riders headed to the fort for more Long Knives.

Helga watched with growing love as the young lieutenant stood calmly near the front line, coolly watching the savages whirl by as their attack struck the unyielding defense the Army presented. She felt the same warm, silky moistness that had accompanied her first sight of the brave young officer. Father would not approve, she thought, but she could not fight the hunger that she felt for the brave leader fighting so well down below.

Corporal Murphy spit a wad of chewing tobacco, then sighted a redskin with his carbine. Hell, he thought, he'd seen worse at Pea Ridge. Waves of blue bellies charging into Confederate cannon and bayonets. Of course the Injuns were better fighters than the Yankees. But surely any Southerner worth his fourteen dollars a month could hold off a whole tribe of the best the hostiles could offer.

Fightin' Irishman he was, by God. And so, by all that was holy, was Michael Delehanty Morrison. A flood of warmth and affection flowed out of him for the crotchety first sergeant.

Estillman watched one settler pump round after round through his Winchester repeater faster than he could sight a target. The young officer shook his head in impatient disgust.

"Hey!" he finally shouted and walked up next to the crouched defender as the melee swirled around them. "You gonna point that thing or is it just for making noise?"

The farmer turned a blank face to Estillman. "I'm tryin' as hard as I can, Lieutenant," the rattled civilian answered defensively.

"Look," Estillman began as he came to one knee next to the shooter and pointed out at the swarm of Indians. "Choose a target," he went on. The settler paused and looked out to where the officer pointed. "*See* your enemy. Hate his guts. Get him in your sights . . . and shoot him dead."

The Winchester fired and a horse buckled under the strike, throwing its rider beneath the hoofs of other ponies that promptly crushed the life out of the brave.

One-Eye looked back where Wild Dog sat on his pony and the second in command felt reassured because he could see his leader rocking while he sang. This assault was the first of many. It told One-Eye much about who he fought, and he grudgingly gave the soldiers credit for bravery. He leveled his Winchester and caught a trooper in the forehead. He had to remember to tell his warriors to aim for the troopers. Although they did not carry the best weapons, they were the best shots. He cried out and headed back toward his leader.

Suddenly the Indians fell back in a swirl toward the gulley they had sprung from.

At sight of the retreat, Johnny Baxter squinted over the ledge of the gulley. "What the hell they stop for?" he inquired of the wind.

From down below, where he sat on one of the wagons the boys had brought along with ammunition they figured Wild Dog would want, Bobby Baxter closed one eye and studied his brother.

"They know what they're doin'," he commented. "They've done this before."

"You better hope," Johnny answered back. "Or else we're gallows bait."

Estillman looked to the setting sun. Already the light of the day dimmed and the orange color tinted the landscape. "First Sergeant," he called out. The portly Irishman came running.

"Is it true what I've read about the Indians preferring not to fight at night?"

"No, sir," Morrison answered. "Unless when they figure they've got time."

"What do you think?" Estillman inquired calmly as he looked to the west. "Are they done for the day?"

"One more charge and then I think they'll call it quits 'till morning," the first sergeant answered. "We ain't goin' anywhere and Wild Dog knows it."

Holten skirted the large bodies of warriors that rode to combat, then pushed the Morgan to a froth along sweet-smelling stretches of creeks and prairie grass. Time could be counted by the bullets being expended against the beleaguered E Troop. Eli's wounds hampered his goal to find the *Ihoka*. He ended up walking his horse and his burned armpits ached anew. He tried to eat some jerky, but his appetite slowly faded with his strength. The terrain began to change from the flat grassy landscape of the prairie to the forested area of elm, pine and cottonwood. Finally, toward the end of the day, he recognized landmarks he'd noted when he first came this way. Night hovered in the east before he reached the campsite where the scout had met with Two Ponies.

Disappointment darkened his mood as he broke into the clearing, although he already suspected it, not spotting outriders or sentries. The campsite stood deserted. Two Ponies had moved on.

Exhaustion dragged on every bone and the scout shivered as though out on a cold, wet night. Sleep would feel good, Eli thought. Not much, only a little . . . enough to be able to move on. No! he commanded himself. That way lay defeat. Then he spotted the deep groves of several travois.

The two rows of marks left by many of the baggage carriers stood out clearly in the ground. Holten dismounted and examined them closer. Not more than six . . . maybe eight hours old. The edges had not yet begun to crumble. From the depth of the ruts, he estimated all eleven lodges had moved together.

Probably that morning, he added. He could follow them easily, even at night. He took a long swallow from his canteen and girded his flagging body and senses for the long hours ahead.

He tracked them into the fading light and by starshine after that, for more than three hours, gaining half an hour on them with each passing sixty minutes by his estimation. To Eli's relief, Two Ponies headed due east. The Badger Lodge route of march would take them directly to Wild Dog and E Troop.

A charged thickness suddenly filled the air. Holten looked to the sky and could see nothing. He chided himself for letting his fatigue and concentration on the trail prevent him from being aware of the ominous buildup. The stars and moon were nowhere to be seen. Suddenly an eerie shaft of lightning burst from the sky and sent shivers of light through the country. The scout looked about the sparsely wooded area and urged Sonny forward away from the danger of the lightning-drawing trees.

The way Eli figured, it was a sign. He couldn't move in the storm, the trail would soon be obliterated. All he needed now was some place to shelter from the downpour that would break at any second. In the repeated flashes of the thunderbolts, he guided on a low mound that protruded from the buffalo grass ahead. Suddenly the deluge dropped on him, an icy sheet of needles, driven by enormous gusts of wind, blinding his eyes and setting Sonny to skittering. Slowly he gained on the hump in the earth.

His hopes had not been ill-founded, he discovered, when the next bolt of sizzling whiteness illuminated the prairie. An old, abandoned soddy formed the low rise, its once-sharp dimensions blurred and softened by rain and winter freezing. Holten urged speed from Sonny, who slithered on the greasy gumbo mud of the trail. He

173

reached it and dismounted.

Holten checked the interior by match-light, then returned and urged his horse through the partially collapsed entrance. Sections of the roof had given way and water streamed in, yet it provided shelter of sorts from the storm and protection from the electric shafts from the sky. For the tired, sleepy, aching scout, it was time to lie down and partake of rest. He unsaddled Sonny and fed him a sparing handful of oats from a small gunnysack in his possibles bag. He rolled his blanket out in a dry corner of the half-underground house and eased out of his boots. He fell instantly to sleep, his saddle for a pillow.

Outside, the thunderstorm pelted the ground all night. Eli awoke the next morning dry and much refreshed. He felt a thousand times better. Some jerky and hardtack tasted like buffalo hump that early dawn and sated his hunger urge for at least a while. He knew, though, that soon he'd have to get some real food or suffer for his lack of care.

As he feared, the trail no longer existed, pounded out of existence by the gully-washer. It took only a little common sense and a knowledge of the terrain to provide him with a course. If Two Ponies meant to head east to find Holten or the troopers, then the band of warriors, their women and children would favor a particular route. One much the same as taken by E Troop.

Eli wondered if Two Ponies might stumble onto Estillman by accident. No, he reasoned. Women, children, tipis and travois slowed the band too much. The only way Two Ponies could get his warriors to the relief column in time would be to leave his women behind and ride like madmen. Otherwise, they would arrive in time only to bury the bodies.

Sonny had also rested well in the soddy. The Morgan's strength once again dominated the animal's every move and the two travelers pressed forward. Not until mid-day did the scout finally spot the column of warriors led by Two Ponies.

The war chief greeted Eli with a granite face that still suggested admiration. They clasped hands, then Two Ponies spoke what lay foremost on his mind.

"Tall Bear, you do not look well."

Eli wasted no time. He told chief what had happened to him after leaving the *Ihoka* camp, how Wild Dog had tortured him, his fight and escape. He ended with the desperate situation the troop and their charges had been in when he came seeking the Badger Lodge's aid.

Two Ponies nodded and seemed to age as Holten spoke.

"Our time for stopping Wild Dog is growing short. We must ride quickly and aid the Long Knives and the people with them. Otherwise the whole territory will explode in a bloody war."

"If we leave our families unprotected," Two Ponies objected, "Wild Dog might find them and fall on them when we are not here."

"If Wild Dog succeeds and massacres the Long Knives, your families will be no safer from him," Eli countered. The war chief frowned and shook his head.

"First, let me take care of you. We will talk as we eat and my women tend to your wounds."

During the night, Estillman gave the civilian men a quick course in volley fire and bolstered their spines with things to do to improve the defense. He visited the wounded, talked to the troopers and reassured the women and children. He seemed to be everywhere and tireless. Abner Leary observed this, and how troopers and civilians alike looked up to the lieutenant. He felt a burning twinge of jealousy. Why couldn't he be like that? Unconsciously, Abner straightened his shoulders and tried to quell the trembling he felt inside. He followed Estillman on the remainder of his rounds.

"Is everything all right?" Lt. Estillman asked the Brunnens as the patriarch meticulously cleaned his Spencer repeater and double-barreled shotgun.

"Now it is," Helga answered as she leaned toward him. Again her cleavage bulged from her dress, although this time it was not on purpose.

Estillman stared down at the voluminous flesh that filled the girl's blouse and swallowed hard. "Good," he managed in a gruff burst before moving on.

Wild Dog waited for morning, feeling strangely ill at ease. The tumultuous thunderstorm had turned the ground to a slimy morass that would hazard the ponies in their charge. That gave his enemy an advantage they didn't need. He must have some clever strategy that would give the upper hand back to him, like Johnny Baxter's insistence on bringing along two wagons of extra ammunition. Wild Dog had little use or understanding for the white man contraption, yet he appreciated the benefit it represented. When the pony soldiers ran out of ammunition, they were out. His men needn't face that problem. Even so, the rolling wood lodges had caused more difficulties.

His braves had been put to work to haul the rolling wood and the Baxter boys out of the gulley to escape a flash-flood that boiled down on them. Wild Dog sighed, feeling queasy again, and ate another dream-walking pill. At daybreak, Wild Dog attacked again.

This time, the settlers joined in on the volley fire that worked so effectively the day before. The morning consisted of charge after charge that slowly whittled down the resistance of the white men. The attacks took on an unreal quality, the mud reducing each wave of warriors to a trot, rather than whirlwind gallops. Wounded screamed in agony from the clouds of arrows, some tipped with fire, that left the women in the rear

176

guard struggling to fight the flames in trees and shrub. It finally became clear to Loren the simple plan Wild Dog intended to use against him.

Warriors he had, enough to spare, apparently, the way he ran them into burning volleys of lead. Wild Dog also seemed to have plenty of ammunition, food and water. Estillman had plenty of the latter two. What he lacked in this crucial battle of attrition was an ample supply of cartridges and replacements for those who fell in the fight. Estillman wondered if Wild Dog had studied Sherman's march to the sea. When the latest slithering charge of howling savages ended, he again made his rounds of the camp.

Grimly the defenders counted their shrinking supply of bullets and growing number of wounded. Estillman passed among them, hoping against all odds that Holten had made it to Fort Rawlins. Man called out for water and young boys came running with canteens that some troopers had dared in the night to carry to the creek behind the bluff. Estillman recalled how several times Wild Dog had sent braves around back on foot to strike across the water. On each attempt, the clear area of the creek bed afforded the defenders a good field of fire and the sharper rise on their side made a mounted assault near impossible. Estillman found himself wishing the devils would try back there again, so he could send men down to gather up the weapons and ammunition off the bodies of the warriors who would surely be thick on the banks. The sun began to slide down the long afternoon sky to the west again.

Solemnly the defenders checked their meager supplies of cartridges and Loren studied the east with his field glasses. If relief was coming by forced march—say four troops with three remounts per man—the advance elements should have made it by now. He turned to his first sergeant.

"I'm assuming the scout was intercepted," Estillman stated flatly to Morrison. "We're on our own."

"That's hard news, sir. Because I'd say we have enough ammunition between the lot of us for one more good donnybrook. Half the men are wounded and quite a few dead. I'm afraid we can't continue to fight like this."

For the first time, Loren Estillman felt the gut-churning torment that Leary confessed to and all the others showed in their faces. Only he, Morrison and Murphy maintained outward calm. All the same, he now faced his first bout with fear, something he could honestly say he'd never really experienced before.

"What should we do to best insure the survival of the women and children, First Sergeant?" Estillman made an effort to ask calmly.

"Keep the wee ones out of the line of fire, I suppose, sir. After the heathens break our line, there's not much we can hope for. We know they took children from that wagon train. Their lives would be hell that way, but at least they would be alive. As for the women . . ." Morrison trailed off with a helpless shrug.

"No way of stopping that?"

"You know better, sir," Morrison gently chided.

Suddenly the dreaded scream of charging warriors split the air and the now familiar horde erupted out of the gulley.

"Why don't we make a break for it?" a frightened farmer yelled nervously from behind a wagon.

"Any man runs and I'll shoot him dead," Estillman shouted.

"Stay in the line," Morrison roared. "If ye gotta die, do it with a little bit o' dignity."

"That's stupid!" Abner Leary wailed. "There's no way of dying with dignity."

"Oh, yes . . ." Estillman countered forcefully, his eyes ablaze, Colt in hand, ". . . there is."

178

Chapter Sixteen

A boiling mass of warriors filled the ground before the wagons, already nicked and bludgeoned by bullets, arrows sticking from the wood.

"Prepare to fire!" Estillman shouted.

"Guns to the ready, me buckos," Morrison sang out. "Make every round count."

The rolling wave, even more invincible this time as the warriors sensed victory, thundered toward the weakened defense. Their war cries rippled the air with their intensity. They knew the spot where the white men would first fire. A row of dead horses and trodden bodies marked it and young braves vied to get ahead of all their peers so that they could have the honor of leading the charge past that point. They broke across it and Estillman hesitated a second longer than before, hoping for a better chance.

"Fire!" he roared as best his voice would allow.

Morrison also shouted the command, but no one heard his cry. Their rifles and carbines roared out at the charging warriors and once again, as if following a never ending circle, the first file of horses splattered onto the turf, legs flailing, pitching their riders under the hoofs of the charging beasts behind.

Somehow, perched atop his appaloosa, Wild Dog smiled. The Long Knives' fire seemed like raindrops on his warriors. His magic would protect them. They would die, only to rise again. Three opium balls helped foster his version of the slaughter. Even though the charge broke to both sides of the wagons near the brow of the hill, he knew that only a matter of time stood between him and absolute victory. He lifted the strange see-far glasses and studied the fight at closer quarters.

Several braves got past the brush-line barricade and jumped the tongues of wagons, running wild behind the defense positions. For a while the cavalry, detailed to direct civilian fire, controlled their numbers. Soon too many swarmed inside the half-circle to be dealt with quickly.

One-Eye bounded his horse past the soldiers and wasted no time there. He charged up the side of the hill hoping to distract fighters from the wagons, giving more of his brothers a chance to get in and further disrupt the white man's position. Into the copse he went and used his lance to catch a screaming woman between her breasts. He howled victoriously as blood gushed from his victim's mouth.

Helga's father had taken his Spencer repeater down to the line. He left Helga and her mother with his double-barrel shotgun.

Suddenly One-Eye realized only women waited back here. If he got the women to screaming, surely a large number of the white men would come to their rescue. He began to fire arrows wildly about the trees. The noise and sudden stabbing of the shafts into the ground or wood brought shrieks of terror from women nowhere near the danger and proved more powerful than a hit would be.

Helga would not have understood the ploy. All she knew was that her mother sat shivering hysterically next to her and that the wild red man was not like the rude but harmless braves who visited her father. The big girl stood. She palmed back both hammers of the Greener, stepped out from behind her cover and raised the weapon quickly to her shoulder.

One-Eye turned, yelled his war cry to the sudden motion at his side and looked down both barrels of a 12 gauge.

Helga didn't hesitate. She pulled both triggers and felt the big weapon slap brutally against her shoulder and right breast. She stumbled back and completely missed the result of her action.

Her shot hit low, about waist level of the warrior. His pony caught a large portion of the buckshot. They peppered the animal's ribs, except for a clear spot where One-Eye's leg dangled. One-Eye's thigh shattered under the pressure of being pinned against a wall of hard flesh while a mallet of buckshot pounded it. A third of the double-aught pellets went higher.

One-Eye's belly pulped and spilled its contents against a nearby tree trunk as the lead balls broadsided him. His kidneys and intestines spit blood and foul smells through suddenly numerous holes. The blast lifted the warrior off his mount and threw him next to the tree where his innards had landed. The pony ran away, whinnying in agony.

Murphy caught a slug in his shoulder that wheeled him around and threw him hard to the ground. For a moment he struggled to stay conscious, then absently spit a wad of his tobacco as he struggled to a seated position. A quick inspection showed it to be a horrible shot that broke his collarbone. He still felt numb, though, and he one-handed tried to reload his carbine. Let the heathens come, he thought. He'd show 'em.

Estillman dodged the war lance a brave on horseback stabbed at him, ducked inside the strike and slashed through the mounted Indian's arm. The war pony bounded a few feet forward and the short soldier had to leap to stick the point of his sabre into the warrior's kidney. As the corpse crashed downward to join the severed limb, the lieutenant whirled, pointed his pistol and discharged a round point-blank into another charging brave's face. Estillman waved his revolver over his head.

"Back! Fall back to the wagons," he yelled.

For a few moments the attackers seemed not to know what to do next, now that they had breached the wall of the wagons. In that fleeting time, a new cry went up, this one from the west. The troopers and settlers had heard similar yells all day and saw certain death in this indication of reinforcement. The blood-thirsty whoops startled Wild Dog, though, who watched while a new plume of dust swept down across the prairie, made by a long, charging file of warriors. Something about them didn't look right.

Tall Bear, the scout, led them in.

Helplessly, Wild Dog watched as his band of warriors, so close to victory that they stood on it, turned awkwardly to face new enemies. Shouting Oglala braves ran down their flank and rolled across their backs.

Estillman knew instantly what happened when he saw the scout leading the charging Sioux. He jumped onto a wagon, then slashed through a brave's throat when the warrior tried to pull him from the seat. As the dead renegade's head fell off, Estillman shouted.

"Those are Two Ponies' people. They're on our side."

Few heard, since most of the whites were engaged in combat with less friendly Indians. But Morrison caught the gist of it.

"Hey, now," he cried in voice everyone could hear. "An' can ye believe this? The Cavalry is bein' rescued by the Injuns."

Instantly, new heart filled the besieged defenders. The Sioux warriors attacked with brutal precision. Within five minutes, Wild Dog's outflanked followers scrambled to escape.

Not nearly so quickly as their leader did.

He charged back down into the gulley, signaled his most fanatical followers, whom he kept in reserve, to follow. Wild Dog jumped to a wagon full of guns and ammunition. He slapped the animals and the buckboard began to roll along the gulley. Wild Dog only paused long enough to discover the Baxter brothers had been fastest of all to escape.

Eli veered away from the battle once it became obvious the outcome had been decided. He'd seen Wild Dog scramble away. Signaling for several of Two Ponies' men to follow, Eli galloped along the rim of the gulley and quickly spotted the fleeing wagon. He recognized the driver. Holten's Winchester came to his shoulder and he took a shot.

His bullet missed Wild Dog and buried in the spine of one of the draft animals. The sturdy mule squealed in fright and pain and flung back on its hind legs for the last time. The wagon jolted to a violent stop. Only the quick action of one of his escort saved the renegade leader from instant death.

An arm came from Wild Dog's right, before Holten could chamber another round, and the madman swung up onto the back of a loping pony. Quickly the brave lashed his mount to a full gallop. A bend in the gulley cut them off from view.

Eli watched Wild Dog howl off. Tomorrow, the scout swore, he'd get the fiendish monster.

The battle wound down to a sudden, frustrating end. Wild Dog's followers either escaped or died where they stood. Two Ponies' lodge gave no quarter and the whites withdrew as their saviors fell on the fallen renegades. The sense of relief that swelled through the ranks of the rescued seemed palpable as they set about tending properly to their wounded and preparing to move on the next morning. Everybody had lost someone they cared for, but grief was tempered by the simple joy of finding one's self still living. The women began to fix a meal.

Morrison and Eli stood near a tree and watched

Estillman tend to roasting his Arbuckle's coffee beans for the evening's drink. The morose look of defeat had came back to his face.

"I tell ya, he was a wild cat," Morrison bragged, motioning toward the lieutenant. "Kept the line as tight as a dowager's corset, he did. Stood there like nones-the-worry. No one doubted who commanded here." The first sergeant shook his head and walked a distance away, lowered his voice. "And now look at him. Reads that blasted letter one more time an' he's disgustin'."

Eli didn't answer as he pondered the dilemma.

"I wanna know what's botherin' the lad," Morrison insisted in a hoarse whisper. Holten stared into space for a short while before speaking.

"Where's your stash, First Sergeant?" Eli asked simply.

Shortly, the two men approached Estillman, Holten carrying a full bottle of Irish amber. The young officer looked up absently, then did a double-take when he spotted the whiskey.

"It's late, Lieutenant," the scout stated before the commanding officer could say anything. "The sentries are out, Two Ponies' men are camped nearby, and even Leary can handle the situation. It's time you, me and Morrison talked a little . . . alone."

"I don't understand, Mr. Holten," Estillman replied.

"Bring your cup, Lieutenant," Eli pressed.

They walked silently to a small copse of trees a short way inside the ring of sentries. The scout started a small fire in the clearing, then opened the bottle. He poured all around. Morrison looked uncomfortable drinking out a cup instead of the bottle. Estillman stared down into his very full tin, glanced nervously at the two older men as they downed their drinks in one tilt of the head. Loren tried to do the same.

He coughed and sputtered, worked his throat and finished with a gasp.

For a while, they spoke softly about the battle, Morrison stating flatly his pride in his commanding officer's performance under fire. The conversation rambled for some time. Estillman didn't even mention his fiance until he gave up his tin and took to the communal bottle.

"S-she . . . wants me to resign my commission," Estillman blurted out. A thin film of sweat formed on his reddened face. "She wants me to go back to New York and get a job at some trade company, or brokerage house."

"The nerve of her!" Morrison bleated. "Why'd she want you to do a thing like that?"

The bottle of whiskey suffered a predictable fate as Loren rambled some more on the love he had for the woman, her intractable attitude toward frontier life and her satisfaction with the big city. Morrison grudgingly pulled a second bottle from his tunic.

Although he fell over his own words getting his thoughts out on his domestic dilemma, only after a few sips of the new bottle did Estillman even mention his fiance's new beau.

"Th' dee'vil, ya say!" Morrison squeaked out between swallows. "That's a terrible piece of leverin' ta get ye outta the Army. She ought to be ashamed."

Eli remained painfully quiet. He knew there had to be more, as Morrison had said long ago, a piece of the puzzle still missing from Loren Estillman.

"I love her. I do," the lieutenant slurred out. "B-but . . . she says if I really loved her, I'd give up the Army. That it's . . . it's . . . undignified."

"Shameless," the good sergeant intoned sympathetically.

Estillman's face contorted with self-pity as he studied the ground in front of the fire. Then, as though a piece of the flame lit a clear thought in his head, his face gaped with a revelation to shake the ages.

"Hey," he burped. "If she loved *me*, really *loved* me, she wouldn't mind the Army. She'd give a little ground

185

ta me. Think of what I wanted for once."

Now Eli enthusiastically joined the sergeant's drunken argument.

"That's the way you have to look at it," Eli urged. "Some things you have to have for yourself."

A determined, angry expression etched onto the boyish features. Estillman slapped the ground in front of him with an open palm and Morrison quickly retrieved the bottle before Loren could break it.

"Well . . . Fuck her!" Estillman belched, his voice breaking up and down the scale. "Fuck her good. She's never done a damn thing for me but tease my prick. Yeah. Fuck her. Have the whole troop line up and take turns on her. Call out the whole regiment and charge admission. Bring in Two Ponies' braves an' let 'em all have a crack at her."

"I think that's just what she needs," Eli laughed, a clear picture of the 12th Cavalry lined up, patiently waiting their turn on the Philadelphia debutante. "So why don't *you* fuck some sense into her?"

"Oh, I couldn't do that," Estillman lamented. "I'm . . . you see, I'm . . . a . . . virgin."

Everyone sat frozen for a moment. Loren grabbed the bottle back and chugged a healthy large draught, realizing the revelation he'd just made. Suddenly Holten and Morrison saw the light.

"Oooh-hooo," they moaned knowingly in unison.

"You won't tell anybody, will ya?" Estillman pleaded. Morrison winked sagely at Eli, rose as best he could and wandered off.

"Have another drink, Lieutenant," Holten answered. "Your secret is safe with me."

Helga Brunnen huddled under the covers in the back of her father's wagon, unable to sleep with the heat building painfully between her muscled legs. She sighed and tried not to think of her brave, courageous

186

hero, who didn't seem to know she was alive. Instead she thought of killing the warrior that day and shuddered at the recollection. She wondered if her performance under fire would impress the handsome lieutenant. *Verscheisen!* She was back to him again.

Something touched her shoulder lightly as a hand closed over her mouth. She rolled to see the nice first sergeant at her side, practically sitting on her sleeping mother, a finger to his mouth suggesting quiet. She nodded agreement and he released her. He moved with amazing nimbleness for a man of his size as he came off the wagon and motioned for her to follow.

She slipped from the conveyance and joined the Irishman by a tree, grasping a blanket around her ample charms.

"What is going on here?" she demanded.

"I tried to keep it from ya, Miss Brunnen," the sergeant dissembled. His face twisted like rubber into a mournful expression. "Really I did. But now a good man sits, stewin' in his own juices, frolickin' with bad company, swilling them awful spirits an' only a lovin' woman can save him."

The tale the blarney-filled non-com spun could have brought tears to Judge Roy Bean. It included the scourge of a woman who carelessly tossed the young man's affections aside, the tempting tool of the devil, demon rum, replacing the Jezebel in his heart, and the weight of command dragging the young officer down.

"He drinks?" Helga asked astonished.

"Like a fish," exclaimed the sergeant. "I've only just left him now, speakin' temperance, but that ne'er-do-well scout, Holten, tempts him to the bottle."

"Mr. Holten is a bad influence?' Helga again inquired in amazement.

"Oh, my child," Morrison exclaimed like a priest. "The stories you'll hear about that man when we get to the fort. Tiz a crime the way he plays loose with young ladies' affections."

Helga's jaw sagged open. Morrison nodded sadly.

"Vhat can I do?" she asked honestly, her face formed into her saddest expression. "He does not know I exist."

"But he does," Morrison insisted. "He only fears you'll use him up and throw him away, like the hussy that only so recently broke his heart."

In a moment of powerful emotion, the sergeant grasped her broad shoulders and caught her clearly in his eyes, her love-glowing orbs matching his bleary ones.

"He can't perform his duties as an officer of the United States Army if he's under the influence of the bottle. They'll surely court-martial him if he shows up drunk at the fort. I'm not askin' it for me, or even for the lieutenant. I'm askin' it for the safety of the whole relief force. Only you can save us."

Helga's breath shivered through her mouth, caught in the fanciful images Morrison wove. "I'll try," she consented.

Eli loosened his buckskin shirt. Absently, Estillman did the same. The scout pulled off his boots. Without even realizing it, the inebriated officer aped Holten and removed his own.

"The sergeant coming back?" Estillman slurred.

Out of the shadows stepped the ghost of a Valkyrie, hugging a blanket to her chest.

"You will leave now, *Herr* Scout," she ordered with the authority of Valhallah. Eli hesitated only for a moment. He found Morrison behind a nearby tree.

"I only hope the lieutenant has a stout heart and a stouter pecker tonight," Morrison heaved. He smacked his lips several times, turned and walked away without another word.

After a moment of wistful temptation, Eli left the young couple to themselves.

Helga dropped her blanket, exposing a too-sheer

188

nightie stretched to the limit by her voluminous breasts. She fell to her knees in front of Loren. For a moment, they gazed into each other's eyes. Estillman looked like he was trying to stare down a charging bull. Then, without a word, the German maiden pulled her gown off over her head and the lieutenant felt a stirring in his loins.

Helga's flesh was creamy smooth with muscles rippling under the surface. Not a pound of fat rested on her bones. Even her large breasts thrust out at a firm attention, no sag, no sway. Her ample upper structure arrowed to a trim, narrow waist.

"Lord! Those are for real," Loren blurted out before his face got buried in the cleft between the tremendous mammaries.

"I von't leave you, *liebchen*," Helga cooed as she undid the last buttons to the officer's tunic. "I vill be here as long as you vant."

"But, I . . . but . . . I . . ."

Helga put a finger to his lips. "*Ja*, I know. You haff a girl back east who treats you like dirt. Vell, she iss there *und* I am here. Und I love you so much, I ache."

"It's not that, really. It's . . . only . . . that . . . that I've . . . never . . ."

"Neither haff I, mine darling. So, we can learn this vonderful thing together."

Loren suddenly fumbled clumsily with his belt, pulling, then kicking his trousers off.

A large white snake slithered into the scene. Helga sighed in contentment. Loren gaped.

"It's . . . never hurt like that before," he whispered, wonderingly.

Helga could not restrain herself any longer. She grasped her soldier's manhood, sighed at its silky touch, then drew him closer to her with it. The blonde thatch between her strong legs grew moist and quivering with expectation.

"Ohmygosh," Estillman blurted. "Wh-What . . .

are we . . . ? How d-do we . . .?"

"Hush, mine mighty *Ritter* and come to your Helga."
Tenderly she positioned Loren on the ground and sank
her passion-scented flesh down onto his mighty sword.

Pain flared briefly for both of them, then Loren
found his fiery member encased in a soft, moist prison
whose walls undulated with powerful hunger. Tentatively he thrust upward.

Bells rang.

Angelic choruses sang.

All the fireworks of his childhood exploded in the
vault of his head. All the Alpine yodelers of her home-
land shivered the canyons of her mind. Glory succeeded
glory and it seemed to them that the rising pinnacles of
heavenly delight would never end. Of course, all too
soon, they did.

"There now," Helga whispered through the golden
haze that surrounded them. "The first time is over for
both of us. Vasn't it . . . vasn't it vonderful?"

Drawn from his sated reverie, Estillman could only
croon a reply.

By the second amorous encounter, Lieutenant Loren
Estillman was cold sober, on top and in command.

"Don't stop, *liebchen!*" the Valkyrie cried as
Estillman struggled ecstatically to bury his lance to the
hilt. "Nefer stop!"

For most of the night, *liebchen* didn't.

Chapter Seventeen

Mourning doves called sadly through the brisk morning air. Bushytailed red squirrels scolded the homesteaders who stirred about cooking fires and saw to the harness of their teams. Two Ponies and several of his followers joined Holten and Estillman, with his loyal first sergeant by his side, at the far end of the rise from where the wagons waited.

"I am committed to the death of Wild Dog," Two Ponies stated, while Eli translated. "He is not done yet. Although he has lost many braves and others desert him, my scouts have found him, still blocking the trail to the pony soldier's wooden walls."

"We're nearly out of ammunition," Estillman told him. "What are we to do?"

We captured one of the Baxter wagons full of ammunition for those repeaters they sold to Wild Dog," Eli reminded him. "And we've picked up enough of the Spencer repeaters from dead warriors to, if you're willing, arm about half of the troop with them."

"That'll leave enough cartridges for the carbines to give the other half about fifteen rounds each," Morrison added.

Estillman's head throbbed from the unaccustomed amount of liquor he had consumed and his loins ached with a soreness he had never before encountered. In spite of all that, a broad grin shaped his features into a bemused gentleness.

"So, we're not out of ammunition," he said. Then he winked. "Although I don't know how well our report will be received when the Inspector General discovers we rearmed our troop with something other than government issue weapons."

"Let Frank Corrington worry about that," Eli offered.

"Tall Bear," Two Ponies interrupted. "Have you told them how you plan to kill Wild Dog to save the other braves?"

"What was that?" Loren Estillman inquired.

Eli resisted a nervous smile and explained about the plan Two Ponies supported.

Estillman seemed entranced as he tried to listen to the scout's words. Despite the seriousness of their situation and the tone this discussion had taken, he could not rid his face of that wide, sappy smile.

"You gotta be kidding," was all he said.

"What were your marching orders, Lieutenant?" the scout countered gently, and continued without waiting for an answer. "We weren't sent out here to punish anybody. If we kill Wild Dog, we'll end the uprising and that's what we want."

"Yes . . . yes, I suppose we will," Estillman replied dreamily. His eyes focused beyond them on the marvelous form of Helga Brunnen. "Do . . . do what you think right. Carry on, Mr. Holten."

"May the saints protect us all," Morrison said wonderingly after the lieutenant walked away in the direction of the light of his life. "Sure an' we git him proper laid an' he turns into a pussy-cat."

An aching need grew torturously in Wild Dog's body. He took more and more of the dream-walking pills and he hardly ever felt good. His numbers had shrunk by a third, but still his song — and the magic pills — made strong medicine. All he need do is sing harder and those that had fallen in battle or left in fear would return.

He was not done with the pony soldiers. He still blocked their path east. They still ran low on ammunition for their carbines. A day to regroup, strengthen the resolve of his men, and he would strike again. This time the men of the Badger Society would die right along with the whites. The demented war chief could hear excitement outside, the barking of the camp dogs and the trundling of wagon wheels. He left his lodge to greet the returning shadow-men.

Johnny and Bobby Baxter flashed no sun from their teeth today. They hadn't a happy thought in their heads after what had happened yesterday. They reined up the team in front of Wild Dog's lodge.

"So," the angry warrior greeted coldly. "You who first ran away choose to return. Why should I welcome you?"

"We've thrown our lot in with you, Wild Dog," Johnny evaded from the seat of the wagon. "Right now, we don't have much else we can do."

"Where's our other wagon?" Bobby asked as he looked around the camp.

"Go ask the pony soldiers," Wild Dog answered with a crooked smile.

"You left it behind?" the elder Baxter blurted out. He straightened his shoulders and jumped from the high seat to step in front of the powerful war chief.

"My brother and I just spent the entire night pickin' our way through the dark to get to our cache to bring you more ammunition and firewater and this is how you repay us?"

193

Instantly the medicine maker felt a pang of guilt for doubting the loyalties of his mentors.

"You fled away when the *Ihoka* attacked . . ." he countered weakly.

"We weren't gonna be much use to you there, Wild Dog," Johnny returned soberly. "And no, we weren't gonna hang around to die with you. As you can see, none of us are dead, although some of us are poorer." Two sets of red, watery eyes stared into each other for a long second before Baxter sighed.

"What's done is done, I guess," he relented philosophically. Johnny walked back to the wagon and pulled the tarp back to reveal boxes of ammunition and cases of cheap, cayenne-and-tobacco flavored white whiskey bulking on the wagon bed.

"We've brought you a present," Baxter offered. "Can yuh pay for it?"

All day the relief column prepared for the offensive. All thoughts of pulling out of the haven of trees were forgotten as scouts reported back that Wild Dog still controlled all trails back to Fort Rawlins. The troop farrier labored on the horses to insure all were properly shod for battle. The troopers still capable of riding checked and cleaned their weapons, inspected their carbine rounds or familiarized themselves with the new weapons taken from the enemy.

Meanwhile, Estillman—somewhat more himself after a breakfast with Helga—and Two Ponies wrangled over incidentals. Both agreed that they should attack early the next morning.

"We must attack soon, so that the defeat Wild Dog suffered yesterday will be fresh in his followers' minds. They must have some doubt about their leader, even as we speak."

"You are wise, Two Ponies. I have maybe fifty men who can mount and ride in an assault," Loren stated after hearing Eli's translation. He industriously ground his own beans in the buttstock grinder of a Coffee Mill Sharps he'd picked from the battlefield as a souvenir, while he drank a cup of previously brewed coffee.

"You're going through your whole ration of Arbuckle's, Lieutenant," Eli noted humorously.

"Believe me," Estillman said with a rub at his forehead, "I need it." He pointed at the drawing in the dirt the scout had made of the location of the hostiles. "Mr. Holten proposes that E Troop make a frontal assault. If fifty soldiers riding straight into their faces doesn't bring out the eighty or so Indians still following Wild Dog, nothing will. I concur with that. And I think I have a means of making that more effective.

"Two Ponies can sneak men into position tonight along the gulley on the right and the left fork of the creek. If they keep out of sight until the proper moment . . . Well, I think we can provide Wild Dog with a surprise he's not seen in his dream-walking. Then, Holten, with your skirmishers hitting his rear, the trap should be complete. It's an old battle plan, by a Carthaginian general nearly two thousand years ago."

Eli translated for the war chief, who nodded sagely.

"But you, Tall Bear, will be the one who will end this thing for good," Two Ponies summarized. "As long as Wild Dog lives, young men will answer his song with their blood. As the soldier chief says, you will go to the south, take a handful of my best warriors, and approach from the rear when all his men are busy fighting us. As you told me, you will locate his war council, where Wild Dog will be directing the battle. You must be sure to kill him, Tall Bear. Then the braves who have ridden with him will seek their families again."

Holten translated this back to Estillman, who nodded to Two Ponies.

"I'll go along with that, for expediency's sake. Though all we need is the diversion in the enemy's rear to complete the impression of total defeat," Estillman agreed for form. Then his voice turned hard. "But, I'll tell you this. If those boys ever leave their families again, to make war on the whites, the Army is going to tan their hides for sale to Easterners to wear as coats."

All that remained to be done for the relief force was to ready the defenses of the settlers being left behind at the trees.

Wild Dog's braves found better things to do.

While the drug-maddened fanatic whipped them into a religious frenzy, his warriors drank copious amounts of the rot-gut whiskey supplied by the Baxter brothers. Johnny stayed close to Wild Dog's side, feeding him more of the opium pills, eating a few himself. The war drums sounded louder and louder as the warriors gained strength and bravery from their peers and leader.

"Gonna attack tomorrow?" Johnny inquired. Wild Dog shook his head.

"Time is on my side. My scouts reports no one comes from the pony soldiers' place to the east. The last battle is still too fresh in my warriors' minds. Some will prove their courage tomorrow by playing with the trapped whites. They will ride out of rifle range, taunting the enemy to come out."

"What if the pony soldiers make a break for it . . . or attack?"

Wild Dog smiled at the thought.

"Then we will wipe them out as they run. I still have many more men than they do, even with the *Ihoka* in their midst."

Johnny thought a moment as Wild Dog ran from warrior to warrior, singing and chanting, urging the braves with religious fervor. At last Johnny went to him.

"Say, ya know, me an' Bobby have some buffalo rifles. We can maybe kill a couple of the Long Knives from a great distance. At least drop their horses, from the gulley, without any chance of them catching us."

Wild Dog thought about that for a moment, a maniacal grin on his face.

"You should do that right now," he answered.

"I'll wait 'till tomorrow, if ya don't mind," Baxter hastily countered. "I'm purely tuckered after last night's ride."

To the constant throb of stiffened bullhide drums and the serpent call of buffalo hoof rattles, the frenzied dance of the warriors went from being a contrived attempt at bravado to hard-felt hysteria. By nightfall, many young braves ached to ride on the besieged column and swarm over it right then. Wild Dog knew that with another day of dance and whiskey, they would have forgotten the defeat they'd suffered.

Then . . . then, he vowed, his band would sweep over the white-eyes like a thunderstorm.

Chapter Eighteen

The Oglala women and children arrived with their limited escort of older warriors an hour before nightfall, much to the relief of Two Ponies. With their families safe, nothing stood in the way of the plans Estillman and the Oglala war chief had made. The tipis were erected within the circle formed by the wagons and trees. The Indian allies' families would suffer the same fate as the settlers if the Army attack failed.

Morning broke with shades of red and orange over the waving buffalo grass to the east. The troopers had already set about saddling their horses and checking their weapons one more time. Eli, with Two Ponies' picked warriors had long ago left in the dark, preparing to fulfill his part in the plotted attack. Only eight warriors rode with Estillman's column, dressed regally in flowing bonnets. They led the way to the field that spread out in front of Wild Dog's camp. The column formed an unusual 'V' formation, the center thrusting out ahead of the flanks. The *Ihoka* warriors spread out into the meadow, taunting Wild Dog's followers to attack.

Wild Dog's camp boiled in bedlam over the unexpected opportunity. Howling warriors ran about as they snatched up their weapons and leapt to their ponies. Camp dogs yapped hysterically with the excitement. Soon a frothing sea of horses stomped impatiently, waiting for a sign of direction.

Wild Dog knew his song had reached its crest. The

Long Knives came against a larger force, to be slaughtered in an open field. He could see a group of warriors prancing out in front of the pony soldiers.

"There were over thirty braves with Two Ponies before," one of his councilors pointed out.

"They have fled before my song," Wild Dog proclaimed jubilantly, "and the white devils come to sacrifice themselves to it in the open. This morning we will wade in blood and crush the pony soldiers. This afternoon the white women will satisfy our loins."

While Wild Dog spoke, the cavalry marched two thirds of the distance across the field, bugle blowing. Their long knives clattered like gnashing teeth. Sergeants bellowed across the waving grass. Except for a few older warriors, who stayed stoically with the lieutenant, the young Oglalas rode practically to the base of the elms Wild Dog had camped under.

"There!" Wild Dog shouted, one strong finger pointing to a volunteer who wore Two Ponies' war bonnet and regalia. "There is Two Ponies with the Long Knives' war chief." The mad grin that the renegade leader had lacked since the defeat at the hands of the Oglala returned with a vengeance. *"Hu ihpeya wichapo!"* he screamed to his men as he flew to the back of his pony. "Humiliate the enemy."

At the command, the cavalry quickly dismounted, every fourth man held the horses for the three that stepped forward and went to a knee. They fired accurate volleys at the swarming mass of hostiles that raged out of the trees. The troopers let the enemy approach to twenty yards, then the center of the protracted line began to fall back, giving ground gradually, as though hard pressed. Wild Dog's men quickly rushed into the vacated space. They swarmed forward, hungry to meet the enemy in hand-to-hand battle.

Satisfied that the white-eyes had broken, Wild Dog and his war council withdrew to a nearby rise to watch the battle. To the right of the doomed troopers ran the gulley that had afforded the renegades a covered route of approach to their attack on the settlers. To the left stood several lonely trees and a shallow creek, with narrow, steep banks. Wild Dog knew victory rode with his song. They provided no escape for his enemies. He began to chant.

Eli took the men Two Ponies had suggested. No young warriors rode with them. The braves the Badger leader had given him were hard, experienced fighters who seemed resolute instead of glory seekers, grim instead of drunk with expectation. Probably all fathers, Eli thought.

Eli and his men left an hour after midnight, shortly after Two Ponies, headed south instead of north. The main body of warriors slipped into the gulley and along the creek bed, while Eli and his five men skirted the whole area and came up to a place behind the renegade camp a half hour before dawn. The small contingent hid in a sparse grove of trees. Eli directed the horses to be put on ground tethers to graze and waited with his men for the attack to begin.

Loren Estillman stayed on his horse near the failing center as it withdrew. The flanks quickly became thinned and overextended. The renegades knew they stood the best chance against the organized troop by breaking it up into smaller pockets and bringing the men to hand-to-hand combat, for no military force in the world could best the American Indian at that. For this reason, they put their greatest pressure on the weakening center of Estillman's line.

Unfortunately, the cavalry did not cooperate. Instead, recall sounded and the troop regrouped before they contineud to fall back. One horse reared as an arrow penetrated its withers and pulled the reins of the other three mounts from the trooper trying to hold them in place. The raddled animals bounded toward the rear, leaving the soldiers suddenly isolated in the face of the charging warriors.

Estillman bellowed like a rutting buffalo, drew his Colt and charged one of the bounding horses. With the seven-and-a-half inch barrel of the revolver he hooked the horse's reins from under its neck and worked the leather lead into his hands. Then he charged toward the four quickly fading troopers.

"Fall back with the troop," he commanded and handed the reins to the horse handler. "Go get those other mounts."

The shrieking Indians, whose charge had nearly been broken by controlled volley now surged deeper into the gap left by the retreating soldiers. The hole, they knew, would break the dismounted cavalry in half and that would be the end of E Troop.

An arrow struck one trooper square in the chest, split through the ribs, punctured a lung and his liver. He spewed blood from his mouth as he screamed.

The breach widened.

Suddenly Estillman's mount jumped into the gap. He leapt from its back as the transfixed trooper fell dead at his feet. The lieutenant bent down to pick up the dead man's carbine when another beefy palm beat him to it. Loren raised his eyes to a kindly scowling Sergeant Morrison.

"Lieutenant," Morrison chided. "I'm shocked. No . . . *disappointed.* I thought ye knew better." The sergeant pointed to the blood-stained dirt as the surviving troopers scrambled for the horses that the handler brought. "This is trooper's work, sir. Beggin' yer pardon, but I'll speak to ye later about this. Ye'll kindly get back to yer position an' I'll not tolerate any more foolish bravado."

Estillman opened his mouth to argue when an arrow whizzed between the officer and his first soldier. It seemed a wise time to fall back.

Eli eased over a fallen tree. The *Ihoka* braves slipped around and under it as they followed the ridge line. Holten could see Wild Dog and his war council, eyes fixed on the battle that raged below them.

Suddenly riders closed in on the little band from the east. Wild Dog's reserve, who charged through the sparse trees screaming their battle cries as they wielded war clubs that whirred through the air past Eli's head as they thundered by.

"They should be out of bullets," one suspicious councilor noted about the soldiers below.

"Where could they have gotten more ammunition?" Wild Dog taunted back, though in his troubled heart he knew. The pony soldiers used Spencers, like those brought him by the Baxters. Stripped from the dead, who had not come back at the summons of his song, and the soldiers had a wagonload of ammunition for them.

The battle focused on the center of the line, now a sunken bowl with the mounted flanks keeping the battle contained inward. Wild Dog's warriors flung themselves on the troopers they now over-ran.

Then the trumpeter sounded a signal.

Two Ponies saw the wisdom of the plan worked out by Tall Bear and the soldier chief. The renegades looked away from their hand-to-hand struggle with the troopers to see Two Ponies and a dozen of his men ride howling from the gulley. Another twelve rose up from the creek and this surprise force fell on their enemy from both flanks.

Pandemonium replaced confidence for Wild Dog's followers. Two Ponies' mounted braves raced through the entrapped renegades and, with war lances, skewered the dismounted Indians. The troopers fired point-blank into the raddled kill-song chanters. Wild Dog's braves ran for their ponies, escape the only option they enjoyed.

"Trumpeter," Estillman shouted from the once-failing center. "Sound the charge!" And the young officer's voice did not crack once.

Crisp notes burst from the bugle as the troopers vaulted to their horses' backs. Suddenly the battle had turned.

Eli fired a skin-contact shot into a brave who leapt from his mount as the scout blocked another man's tomahawk. Then Holten swung around, leveled his Winchester and fired another round into the back of the warrior who had ridden past him with the war club. For the five hard, cold *Ihoka* fighters, the remaining young braves posed little trouble. One chant-singer bounded onto a middle-aged warrior, who slammed a hard palm into the attacker's chest before twisting the brave's own knife up into the younger man's stomach. The luckless hostile fell against a tree, the knife buried in his spleen. The Oglala delivered a final crushing blow to his dying enemy's cranium with a high-arching strike from his stone war club.

The skull splintered like an over-ripe gourd, blood and fluid bursting loose with gory pieces of flesh, bone and brain. The final attacker tried to ride off to warn Wild Dog. An arrowhead burst out between his upper ribs as the arrow fletchings quivered in his back. He straightened tightly, arched with pain, before he fell from his horse, dead at the brow of the hill.

"Seize their horses," Eli commented. Any hope of surprise now rested in speed and with Wild Dog's preoccupation with the disaster unfolding on the field.

An insistent bell-like piping of the bugle acted like a kill-song for the troopers. They drew their sabres and howled like doomed souls as they charged the disrupted hostiles.

"This cannot be!" Wild Dog shouted down at the

debacle below. "I have dream-walked in the light of day, I have seen the white-eyes die like dogs in the sun. This is not how the dreams showed me . . ." Suddenly he craved more of the dream-walking pills. He felt at the pouch in his sash, but his touch told him he was out of the syrupy balls.

"Enough!" one war council member interrupted. "I have heard enough of this song. Call the men back. Let us flee now, or the pony soldiers will hang us like buffalo hides set out to dry."

"Perhaps it is as Tall Bear said," another wise member suggested. "Perhaps the dreams are nothing but Wild Dog's death song."

"If that is so," Wild Dog's insane logic went, "then it is John-nee Bax-ter's doing, for it is his dream-walking pills that showed me this."

The death-singer reined his mount around and headed for the volcano-cones of his tipis. He pushed his steed to the limit, aching to find his mentor in the camp. Baxter lied to him, Wild Dog howled to himself. Perhaps . . . perhaps the Baxter brothers were even whites, not shadow-people as they had claimed to be. The thought brought the now ever-present death song once again to his lips.

Johnny and Bobby no longer resided in the camp. Wagon tracks pointed north out of Wild Dog's war camp. Wild Dog looked around wildly, froth forming on his lips. His body trembled and jerked. Then an old enemy, as much to blame as the Baxters for the medicine man's undeserved defeat, stepped out of the cover of a lodge.

Tall Bear nonchalantly made a rude gesture in sign language that placed Wild Dog's penis in an impossible position and casually threw his rifle and revolver to the side of the tipi. "I am here to kill you, Wild Dog," he announced. "I will do it in the traditional way."

Holten walked deliberately to where the council fire burned the night before. Five Oglala joined him, their

Badger totems worked into their hair.

Wild Dog's war council skidded to a halt next to their leader. Eli immediately regretted his bravado in stepping out to make his one-on-one challenge. The five councilmen faced their enemy in stony silence.

Eli forced himself to ignore everything but Wild Dog. No one else mattered. For once, the coward didn't run as the scout charged his pony on foot.

Wild Dog's maniacal grin rippled across his face, then he flung himself at this enemy, Holten, the new source in his mind for all his problems.

The war chief covered the distance to Holten in one thrust of his legs. Eli suddenly realized the madman was not all show. With the strength of the insane, Wild Dog delivered a sizzling fast slap to Eli's temple. The blow dislodged the scout from the ground and threw him unceremoniously into the side of a tipi. Wild Dog leaned down as his song began to bubble from his frothing lips. He heaved Holten to his feet as though the scout were made of straw. The raving renegade powered a knee upward into Holten's crotch.

Eli swung a thigh to parry the blow with the experience of a thousand fights. Inexplicably, the warrior's knee came through the block and struck Holten an inch from his groin.

Stars flickered by in the splotchy bits of darkness that complicated Eli's sight.

Chapter Nineteen

With unharnessed emotion writhing across his face like he had ants under his skin, Wild Dog pulled his knife. Eli quickly drew his Bowie.

Wild Dog's war council had lost all faith in their leader. Regardless, as outlaws, these Asiniboine warriors saw only death and disgrace facing them. They preferred to meet it as men. With a shout, they attacked Eli's five Oglala stalwarts. Screaming braves closed on each other with knives and tomahawks. All followed their leaders' choice of traditional weapons and threw their guns aside. War cries rent the air. Grunting efforts drew quick blood.

The battle in the field turned into a rout among the outlying trees. Only the most fanatical followers of the insane medicine maker resisted the overwhelming odds.

Neither Eli nor Wild Dog could hear what boiled around them. Wild Dog listened *only* to his song as frothing saliva foamed from his mouth. Holten concentrated on killing the madman who had murdered his friends; Black Spotted Horse, Gray Otter and his sons.

The insanely strong medicine man thrust and Eli yielded to the threat, twisted out of the way and slashed across Wild Dog's belly, an inch away from flesh. The scout recovered, feinted, then stabbed again, this time drawing blood, his Bowie slicing between the bones of Wild Dog's knife arm.

For an instant, Eli wrestled to free his blade from Wild Dog's forearm. The knife ripped loose, severing muscle and one tendon. Wild Dog's hunting knife fell from his hand.

Holten moved in for the kill: Wild Dog looked to the right and behind, where flames licked at the tipis. To the left, troopers and Two Ponies' men swarmed closer. The medicine man grimaced at his opponent, then charged. The scout slashed the Bowie under Wild Dog's left armpit as the incredibly fast madman wrapped both arms around Eli's chest. His left hand grasped his bleeding right forearm.

Wild Dog was a head shorter than Eli, yet the scout's breath heaved out as the maniacal strength of the renegade crushed at his lungs. Holten's spine began to crackle as pressure built quickly and he lost his grip on the Bowie. Eli flailed empty-handed at the warrior's back but could not stop the death-squeeze that threatened to kill him. The scout cupped both palms and spread his arms. With all the strength he could muster, he slammed his hands over Wild Dog's ears. The grunting medicine maker shuddered and his grip loosed a fraction. Once more Eli popped an explosive blow to the demented warrior's ears.

Still Wild Dog only shuddered, though blood ran from shattered eardrums. Then the grip loosened more. Eli broke away and punched Wild Dog in the mouth.

Wild Dog kept his feet. His left hand fumbled at his sash and brought out a steel-bladed trade hatchet. The feather-decorated tomahawk swished through the air and forced Eli to jump back.

"Mine is a power-song," Wild Dog chanted in a curious tone, robbed now of his hearing. "Mine is your death-song."

"Not this time, Wild Dog."

Whistling air accompanied another swing of the 'hawk. Eli dived forward under its deadly arc. His heart pounded and for a moment he wondered if anyone could kill Wild Dog.

Holten's maneuver took him through the crazed

Indian's wide-spread legs in a low roll. The scout came up with his Bowie. He bounded to his feet and turned as Wild Dog charged again.

"*Huka hey!*" Wild Dog screamed.

It *was* a good day to die.

Holten ducked under the overhand swing and buried his Bowie in Wild Dog's belly. The tip angled up so that it pierced the renegade's diaphragm. With a violent twist, Eli freed the knife and pulled it out. Wild Dog staggered backwards.

Although he stood, menacing Holten with his tomahawk, Wild Dog was dead.

His feet kept the carcass suspended long after the new flood channel let his heart pump existence out of him in a crimson tide. Reality finally caught up with Wild Dog and he fell slowly to the ground, his song forever silenced.

Estillman rode wildly into camp, leading the cavalry. Those left of the renegade war council scattered in every direction. Wild Dog's Death-Song uprising lay crushed around its leader while flames spread through the lodges of his camp.

Two Ponies screamed into the camp, victory howls rose from the members of his society.

"Wild Dog is dead," Holten shouted to the war chief.

Two Ponies jumped from his horse to get a better look at the man once considered supernatural. Then he glanced back at Eli. "Tall Bear, you have avenged the Oglala. The uprising is over. You will tell the Little White War Chief that the white men are safe once again?"

"Wasn't that great?" Estillman shouted to no one in particular. He rode in a circle around the camp, Colt in hand, searching the burning lodges.

"Lt. Estillman," Holten called when the officer came around again. "Two Ponies wishes me to tell you that the uprising is crushed and the settlers are safe to return home."

"That's news they'll be glad to hear," Estillman answered. "There's still something to be done, though. Where, Scout, are the two white men who sold Wild Dog all his guns and whiskey?"

"Look, Tall Bear," Two Ponies exclaimed as he spotted the wagon marks leading into camp. "The two white traders have been here."

Holten studied the ground. His sides ached, another torment to add to his many, though he ignored that in his concentration. With Two Ponies and Estillman flanking him, he walked through the ruins. At last he nodded and pointed to deep ruts, pressed into blood-soaked soil.

"And they left. About the time we hit the camp, I'd say. They went north."

The Oglala war chief turned his granite-hard face to Holten. "We have punished the Indians that rose up against the white man's law. You said that if we did this, the two whites who gave Wild Dog the dream-walking pills would be punished as well."

"They will be, Two Ponies," Eli answered. "I swear to you, those two I also seek revenge on."

"And soon as we've mopped up here, we'll go after those boys," Estillman said, not realizing he fell in line with the conversation Two Ponies and the scout were having in Lakota.

"If I may make a suggestion, sir," Eli countered. "Let me go now, you take your time and make sure the settlers are safe, then try to catch up."

"That could take days, Eli," the lieutenant argued.

"The problem is, Loren," Holten continued, stepping close to the officer's horse. "That you've still got a bunch of wild renegades running around here somewhere, thinkin' they're on the warpath. They broke and ran right now, and in a week they'll be home with their families licking their wounds. But they might want to double back and knock down a few more soddies before they're through, just to show themselves they weren't defeated. With, ah . . ." he glanced at the stern-faced Badger leader, "all due respect to Two Ponies' optimism."

Loren frowned and gazed off to the north.

"If that's the case, I can't spare any men to follow you, Eli. I'm down to a third of my strength as it is."

"I'll try to bring them back alive, Loren," Eli said. "But I can't make any promises."

First, Eli had to recover Sonny. The big Morgan grazed patiently outside the fighting area, where Eli and his small detachment had left their mounts. Holten washed himself in the nearby creek, checked the bruises that welted around his chest where Wild Dog had crushed him, then flexed a small meal for himself of dried buffalo, hardtack and water. While he ate, he cleaned his weapons in warm, soapy water, dried and oiled them and reloaded. A careful check showed ample rations for several days and plenty of ammunition. Refreshed and ready, the scout mounted up and headed north along the clearly marked trail left by the Baxter's wagon.

Bobby sniffed as his face grimaced in wallowing pools of self-pity. He scratched at his protruding stomach and sniffed again.

"What the hell's wrong with you?" Johnny snapped at his brother as he held the reins to the two horses.

"Wha'd'ya mean, what's wrong?" Bobby whined back. "We lost our rifles and a wagon and now we ain't gonna make a killing on the uprising."

"We already did make a fortune," Johnny answered. "We have a wagon full of stuff we stole before we left Wild Dog's camp. Better'n eight thousand, I make it. On top of that we must have four thousand dollars worth of gold and silver ol' Wild Dog paid us for what he did buy an' we got away scot-free.

I think we've done all right."

Bobby thought on this for a moment, then a smile played across his face.

"Hell's bells. That's right. With twelve thousand dollars, we can go most anywhere and get to makin' some real money."

"I was thinkin' about some of these gold strikes in the Black Hills we've heard about," Johnny stated. "We could buy ourselves a couple of fine, healthy chippies and start peddlin' them around those camps. Get the girls to lift pokes or find out where the miners're keeping their dust, then we could go down and knock over the claims."

"Gee," Bobby enthused. "That sounds like a pretty good idea. But shouldn't we'd've grabbed some o'those Injun squaws at Wild Dog's camp instead a' spendin' money on white women?"

"Damn! Bobby Baxter, yo're right." Johnny stomped his foot on the wooden driver's box. "Why didn't I think of that while we were still there? Them miners might not take as much shine to a dusky Injun gal, but they'd sure be less cautious about what they said around them. Teach 'em a little English and our fortune would be made." He glanced back over his shoulder.

"I sure hope the Army killed that crazy Wild Dog. Hate ta have him following us."

"What about the *Army* following us?" Bobby asked. The older brother scoffed.

"Now, why the hell would the Army want to bother two honest white traders when they got Injuns to kill?"

The trail stayed clearly marked through the morning as Eli pursued the two brothers. It headed north only far enough to skirt the fighting, then it turned a bit east, aimed for the Black Hills. By noon, the scout could see their dust as the buckboard made good time over the hard ground. He wanted them alive, to stand

211

trial and get hanged. He hoped they had valuables in the wagon from the raids Wild Dog made. Proof like that would slip a hangman's noose around the Baxter brothers' necks.

Once Johnny had allayed his little brother's fears about the financial success of their venture, and spelled out a rosy future, Bobby became worried about keeping it. Using the pair of field glasses they'd stolen back from Wild Dog's lodge, he kept an eye to their rear.

"Damn!" Bobby announced. "We're being followed."

"Don't panic," Johnny advised as he reined the horses in. "Give me the glasses."

"You look, I'll drive," Bobby suggested as he passed the field glasses to Johnny and reached for the splashboard and reins.

"Wait a minute. Hold on," Johnny urged. "We can't outrun riders in a wagon. Let me get a clear look, would you?"

Bobby impatiently fidgeted on the wagon box as Johnny turned and took a long look at the thin bit of dust that rose behind them.

"It's that damn scout, Eli Holten," Johnny cursed. He gazed a little longer. "He's the only rider. There's just one person following us." The Southerner scanned to the sides, looking for more riders overtaking them. After two long minutes he sighed in relief.

"That's it. One rider. Bobby, get out the buffalo guns."

Bobby Baxter pulled the long-barreled Sharps rifles from their leather cases, checked them for cleanliness. The two brothers chortled with excitement as they steadied the horses, securing them by a lead ground anchor, and set their weapons on shooting staffs made especially for the long rifles to rest on. The positions they selected partially hid them behind the buck-board. Carefully the disreputable pair adjusted the sights for distance. Johnny took four hundred yards, Bobby, the better shot, took five hundred. Over the notch-and-wedge sights, they peered at the speck of horse and rider out behind them.

Eli could see the wagon halt. He watched the brothers dismount and disappear behind the 'rolling wood', as the Oglala called the white man's contraption. Holten figured he'd been spotted. He pulled his Winchester and started trotting faster toward the Baxters.

Bobby eyed down the weapon impatiently, his brother taking longer to be ready.

"When I say, 'now,' " Johnny ordered, "We'll fire together. One of us is bound to catch him."

Bobby sneered inwardly. He considered that a waste of powder, primer and lead. The big Sharps rifles would hit at the range they had been set for, not further or closer. He should have shot first, Johnny second, if necessary. But, oh, well, he was the younger brother.

A tense moment passed before Johnny put his right leg back, checked his aim again, then cried, "Now."

The weapons' twin report spooked the horses, although the lead ground anchor kept them from moving. Both brothers yielded smoothly to the recoil of the powerful rifles. They kept the barrels even as they and their Sharps' rocked back from the discharge.

Thunder rolled across the plains.

Eli saw white plumes of smoke rolling over the Baxter wagon. Instantly he jerked Sonny aside and off his feet kicking free of the stirrups and reaching

213

forward to hold the big Morgan's head down.

Not a second too soon.

The first fat .50-120-800 slug ripped up turf ten feet ahead of the two prone figures. The second slug whizzed by overhead, two feet above the belly of the horse. At that range, they had to be Sharps buffalo guns.

Eli figured five seconds to reload those rifles. He couldn't cover five hundred yards in that amount of time. He urged Sonny upright, then mounted and beat a galloping, zig-zag retreat.

"Hey!" Bobby shouted, squinting at the horizon. "Holten's runnin'!"

"Reload your rifle," Johnny commanded. "Then get back on the wagon. We gotta put some distance between us an' him."

The scout circled around. He stayed out of range, urged his mount along the base of slight rises and through occasional stands of trees, until he got ahead of the boys.

Eli hobbled Sonny behind some scrub oak near a small creek, then set himself up at the bottom of a rise in a flourishing stand of tall buffalo grass. Five minutes later the sound of trundling wheels came to Holten's ears.

The Baxter wagon crested the swale and Eli leveled his Winchester on Johnny's chest. He paused, making certain, then squeezed the trigger and the weapon barked a deadly response.

His aim had been off. Firing uphill at a moving target and only estimated range upset Holten's easy kill. The slug whined off the oak brake lever and took the off-wheeler horse solidly behind the right ear. It shuddered the length of its frame as it took one step back, then went to its haunches. A pitiful whinny of pain escaped its frothy mouth before it slid to the ground and dragged its teammate down by the harness that tied them together.

Johnny Baxter didn't pause a beat. He rose with his Sharps and fired a quick shot at the stand of grass. The bullet cut air ten feet above its target.

"Get down there and line up your shot, little brother," he shouted.

Slugs smacked through the grass near the scout when Bobby opened up. Eli thought of killing the second horse. Then he could wait a week until the Army arrived. His plan didn't get a chance to materialize. With the efficiency of a new McCormack plow, a fat .50-120-800 slug ripped up the buffalo grass and soil six inches from his face. Eli fired a quick shot, then lunged back into the grass and slipped away toward a stand of trees.

Johnny threw his little brother his reloaded buffalo rifle. Quickly Bobby set the Sharps on his stand and sighted in one the fleeing figure.

"I think we got him this time, Johnny," Bobby said as he eased the trigger back.

Chapter Twenty

Buffalo hunting is a patient process. A hunter tries to keep from spooking the large creatures so the herd stands and waits for their killer to shoot them all. Time for proper aiming with the adjustable sights is required. Bobby Baxter, in his haste to shoot the scout, did not check his brother's sights. They remained on four hundred yards, where Johnny had left them, when the target, Holten, running for cover was within a hundred yards.

The big gun burst its load of leaden death. Bobby slid evenly back with the recoil. And the bullet spat by over Eli's head, shuddering an elm in the copse Holten ran for. The scout ducked into the cover of the trees.

"Damn!" Bobby cursed, realizing what had gone wrong.

"Never mind," Johnny answered, feverishly reloading the other rifle. "Just reload."

"But he got away," Bobby protested.

"Right where we can keep an eye on him," Johnny crowed with confidence. "We're gonna lob a shot into that bunch of trees every five minutes until it's dark, an' we're gonna keep an eye on any way out so he can't sneak up on us. Like this, we couldn't be safer if we were in the beer garden back at the brewery."

Bobby smiled thoughtfully. "Remember those roses that used to bloom in the spring? It was a regular rose garden, instead of a beer garden."

"Now *that* I miss," Johnny said wistfully. "The rose garden. When it gets dark, we'll double up on the horse and sneak away."

"But we'll have to leave all the things we stole," Bobby whined. Johnny smiled a toothy grin.

"Guess it's good we didn't bring any squaws."

The Baxter boys prided themselves on being meticulous. While Johnny reinforced himself with a little product of the poppy, Bobby watched the grove and every five minutes boomed off a slug into the stand of trees.

As the sun worked its way down the sky, Eli traded his boots for moccasins and shouldered his Sioux bow and a quiver of arrows. He glided back out of the trees and disappeared into the prairie grass. Slowly and cautiously he circled the swale where the Baxter wagon perched. He rushed forward, silently treading the grass. At last he closed on the back of the wagon with the final fading bars of scarlet tinting the western sky. He notched an arrow, then slipped to the edge of the wagon.

Bobby Baxter stood carefully sighting to send another slug at the stand of trees.

"One more before it's too dark to see," Bobby spoke to no one in particular.

Eli drew back the nocking point to the tip of his ear, sighted his target in the fading light across the point of the arrow. His release smoothly flit the shaft into the evening air. It impaled nicely between Bobby Baxter's shoulder blades, the fletching actually penetrating the flesh. The feathers became soaked with blood. Even with Bobby's pudgy thickness the head of the arrow stood well out from his chest.

"Aargh!" he gurgled. Johnny Baxter looked up from the Sharps buffalo rifle he sat holding next to the dead horse still in harness. He screamed when he saw his brother standing silhouetted against the fading light of the west.

Eli leapt from his cover, coming wide around the wagon.

Johnny wildly fired the huge weapon and got propelled over the dead horse for his trouble. He rose and ran screaming into the waving grass of the pairie.

Eli lay flat against the ground, his ears ringing from being so close to the wrong end of the Sharps, the huge slug missing his ear by a foot. Quickly he regained his senses and pursued the surviving Baxter.

Johnny's breath ran wild until he thought he'd die from the stinging lack of air of his lungs. The sight of his beloved little brother brutally killed by the white savage ached his brain. He really could use a few opium pills right now, Johnny thought, but they were back at the wagon. Ragged clarity calmed the Baxter, who set about working his way down to the stand of trees his brother had been sniping at all afternoon. The scout's horse had to be behind the copse, safe from fire, but close enough for the scout to reach quickly.

Sure enough, Johnny found the animal tied to a scrub cottonwood along a narrow creek. He could barely contain his excitement. The scout would have to come this way to continue the search.

Carefully, the Baxter boy began to reload his Sharps, setting the sights on one hundred yards range. Night critters made their usual noises all around him as he settled into the overgrown bank of the creek on the far end, under the scraggly cottonwood where the huge horse calmly stood.

A sudden hush came over the cicadas and crickets.

Johnny Baxter tensed while he quietly raised his long weapon. He thumped back the hammer on the big rifle, rested it against a thick branch and aimed under the Morgan's muzzle.

A moment later the scout appeared, a darker form against the night. Johnny Baxter corrected his aim and knew what triumph felt like. He relished the moment before pulling the trigger.

A calamitous roar came from the Sharps.

The heavy slug struck a tree trunk and, with a low moan, caromed off to shred leaves above Holten's head. The scout had crouched low at the sound of the cocking weapon and now stood, shouting before Baxter had time to reload. "Sonny!"

With a wild scream, Eli's stout, war-trained horse, reared up and smashed hoofs down on the man that crouched next to him. Johnny Baxter's screams of horror and anguish filled the night. Holten rushed to the side of his wildly stomping stallion, but not in time to save the Southern businessman from the wrath of the valiant warhorse.

Sonny drew back, eyes still frantic, skin flinching with nervous energy. He had a look of contempt and disdain for what was left of Johnny Baxter. The shadow-man trader's chest lay flattened, ribs randomly sticking through his shirt, his head and throat stomped into the dirt. Blood oozed out of every hole in the man.

Holten rejoined the troop, riding the Baxter wagon with both their bodies and their stash of stolen goods as evidence in the bed of the vehicle. Sonny looked back over his shoulder to balefully study his master from the harness that restrained the handsome beast. Sonny's whole attitude could be read as, "After all I've done for you . . ."

"Here's enough evidence to close the case right tight, Lieutenant," Eli reported. "If you could, I'd like to put another horse on the wagon before Sonny disowns me."

"It does look a little ridiculous," Estillman admitted.

The trade of horses was made, although Sonny let it be known the incident was hardly forgotten. A stepped-on foot was only one more cross to bear, Holten thought resignedly.

E Troop trudged east, bringing along a few settlers who still wanted to go to the fort. Two Ponies' followers escorted the column. Helga insisted her family complete the journey, much to Estillman's pleasure.

Eli's mood gradually deteriorated as they neared the fort. He had bigger problems there than Wild Dog and the Baxter brothers combined: Sally Sue, White Dove and Samantha Everett. Life could not be worse. Holten's mood built like a thunderhead over him as Fort Rawlins came into view.

Then, as they drew even closer, the sun broke through the clouds for Eli. The morbid thoughts cleared from his mind and his heart soared.

The Hearst wagon train was gone.

The scout rushed toward the gate, urging his Morgan onward. General Frank Corrington sat in a buckboard near the entrance, smoking a cigar and pouring two glasses of well-aged brandy.

"They're gone!" Eli shouted as he reined Sonny up next to the general.

"Don't ever say I've never done anything for you, Eli," Corrington answered.

"How'd you do it?" Eli pressed.

"Ordered them out the minute we heard the uprising was crushed. I've been talking to the wagon-master about how treacherous the passes can be in winter. One good recitation of the Donner party's little bout with a food shortage and the Hearsts were overruled. Everyone left quite quickly."

"How can I ever repay you?" Holten asked sincerely.

The general looked grimly at the scout. "Be careful next time."

Holten feverishly unsaddled and fed Sonny, then handed him over to a stablehand to groom. Once the weight of Sally Sue Hearst lifted, he found a familiar urge swelling in his loins.

Quickly he ran to his cabin, threw the door open and relished the sight of White Doe standing near the stove. The Oglala maiden's eyes lit, then demurely focused on the floor. Eli's breath came rapidly and his buckskin trousers tightened.

"It is good to see Tall Bear again," White Doe murmured. "I have waited for you."

"White Doe . . ." Holten intoned. "A fire burns in me for your company."

The smile on White Doe's face gained a bit of devilment. She turned her back to the scout, and in one tug, pulled the elkskin dress off over her head. Without hesitation, she swung around, fell to her knees and undid Eli's fly. Then she sighed with expectation as she pulled his engorged manhood into the open. As if she had not eaten since Eli last saw her, White Doe hungrily feasted on the food of ecstasy.

"White Doe," Eli breathed heavily. "Your greeting warms my soul." After a long, endearing moment, the scout pulled her back, lifted her from the floor and set her quickly on the bed.

She leaned back to let Holten savor her naked

bronze body as her hand demurely fell to her sparse thatch of jet-black hair and manipulated it to blossom with silky moist petals.

A knock came at the door.

"Wed-ding people!" White Doe angrily spat.

"No," Eli grunted. "They are gone." He ran naked to the window.

Samantha Everett stood patiently at the door, dressed in a clean flowing white dress, with dried wild flowers in her hair.

The door cracked open.

"Hello, Eli," Samantha greeted.

"Umm, ah, Samantha . . . I . . . I . . ."

"Yes, I know," The widow's smile turned to a tinkling laugh. "Little White Doe is in there with you."

Although Eli stood behind the door, one extension of his form bounded out past the concealment. Samantha looked down.

"Dear me!" she exclaimed, glanced around over her shoulder, then grabbed the wandering instrument with her hand as she pushed her way inside.

Samantha smiled a greeting at White Doe, who absently touched herself while studying the new intruder.

"Eli, I came to apologize," she started, not letting go of the head of his throbbing penis. "When I broke in here and saw you with White Doe . . . and Sally Sue . . . all . . . twined into each other, well . . . I spoke like some prude who should be more reserved about judgments. I've been thinking a lot about that night . . . really become . . . quite . . . *obsessed* about it . . ."

"Are you trying to tell me something, Samantha?" Eli asked, the urge aching in his loins.

Samantha let go of Eli and her hands eased up her

frame as she continued. "It's just that . . . well, you are an experienced frontiersman." Her hands grasped her breasts and she squeezed absently as she blushed and stared into Eli's eyes. "Perhaps one should seek to learn from those more familiar with the ways of the wild west."

Her hands expertly loosened her dress and it fell to her hips, exposing her large, firm breasts, their thumb-thick pink nipples hardening with anticipation.

White Doe smiled appreciatively as the woman finished her undressing. The young Oglala looked for another challenger to best.

Then Samantha became a tiger.

Eli lay back on the bed, thinking about his lucky lot in life as the two women greedily ministered to his swollen manhood with hot, hungry lips. His simmering, liquid release bathed them all.

Then youth yielded to the experience of age. Samantha's golden flower blossomed that his stem might enter into her liquid fire-bathed tunnel of lust. She murmured low with delight as that pulsating stalk cleaved her being.

Absently, Eli wondered if something wasn't missing in his life.

White Doe giggled as she ran her small tight nipples along his back and surrounded his ears with them in an attempt to divert him away from the energetic labors of the widow Everett. Her efforts sent shivers of delight through Eli and he plunged deeper into the glory mound beneath him.

A man needed a change of pace every once in a while, he thought as he slowly sidled down the decline from his magnificent peak.

White Doe went to all fours and urged him toward her newly positioned flower. Samantha snuggled up to them, so that her facile tongue could tantalize both fevered organs as they clashed in immortal combat.

He'd soon want to choose a place to winter, the scout continued in his mind as Samantha arms twined around the narrows of his waist while the scout enthusiastically plunged between the slithery petals of the Indian flower and White Doe buried her face between Samantha's wide-spread legs.

He could stay here at the fort. A tempting idea with such versatile company as the two giggling women proved to be. But, civilization had visited recently. Its benefits quite unappealing. The unpleasant thoughts washed away in a tripartite climax of truly magnificent proportions.

Dreamily, he wondered, as the two gorgeous forms nestled in each of his arms, hugging him in their drowsy contentment, what Texas was like that time of the year.